The Berlin Woman

The Berlin Woman

A Novel

Alan Kaufman

Mandel Vilar Press

This book is typeset in MT Waldbaum. The paper used in this book meets the minimum requirements of ANSI/NISO Z39.48-1992 (R1997). ∞

Book design by Barbara Werden
Cover photo/illustration by Sophie Appel

Publisher's Cataloging-in-Publication Data

Names: Kaufman, Alan, author.
Title: The Berlin woman : a novel / Alan Kaufman.
Description: Simsbury, Connecticut : Mandel Vilar Press, [2019]
Identifiers: ISBN 9781942134589 (paperback)
Subjects: LCSH: Jewish authors—Fiction. | Children of Holocaust
    survivors—Fiction. | Man-woman relationships—Fiction. |
    Authoritarianism—Fiction. | Democracy—Fiction. | Jewish fiction.
Classification: LCC PS3561.A827 B47 2019 | DDC 813/.54—dc23

Printed in the United States of America
19 18 19 20 21 22 23 24 25 / 9 8 7 6 5 4 3 2 1

Mandel Vilar Press
19 Oxford Court, Simsbury, Connecticut 06070
www.americasforconservation.org | www.mvpublishers.org

For Norbert Gstrein

*If a person falls freely, he will not
feel his own weight.*
ALBERT EINSTEIN

*Love makes incredible progress; it is a
kind of gangrene of the soul.*
ILYA ILID OBLOMOV,
EPONYMOUS CHARACTER IN
IVAN GORCHOROV'S NOVEL

My gratitude for the dedicated editorial effort of Robert Mandel, Dena Mandel, and Mary Beth Hinton. My thanks as well to John Lane, Erik LaPrade, Rebbie Ratner, Jim Storm, and Bill McCarthy for their constant support during the writing of this book.

Berlin

Chapter 1

On that first fateful night in her Berlin home, just after dinner, as a late-staying unexpected guest, I was invited to abandon the crappy three-night Airbnb rental provided by my Austrian editor and publisher, Elias Schroeder, and sleep over.

I recall how over dinner, after a long and lively chat about our mutual regard for the film director Scorsese, her husband, Hubert, started in his seat when suddenly Lena blurted out with a spooky Hitchcockian trance-stare her insistence that I stay not just for the night but for all three nights that I would be in Berlin. Unsure how to refuse, I glanced pleadingly at Hubert for help but like a beaten dog Hubert wearily agreed and retired early to bed, probably to masturbate at the thought of me mounting his wife.

Lena and I sat up in the kitchen until late, warming to each other, flirting, touching fingertips, she so charming and flattering. When she felt sure that Hubert was conked out in their bedroom she said, "He's asleep. We're alone now," and led me by the hand into her work studio whose immense ceilings and walls held the bitter winter cold like a deep freezer. She threw a dirty nappy yellow comforter over a cot and handed me an authentic, coarse rust-colored Berber robe to sleep in.

"Goodnight," she said indifferently.

"I'm a bit chilly. May I please have a blanket too?" I requested this in a soft tentative squeak as I lay there shivering on the cot, my voice upticked, since among the international yogalike culturati any hint of male self-assertion brands one instantly as a patriarchal macho right-wing asshole.

Her hand waved dismissively, voice disappointed, displeased even. "It's not that bad. The robe is enough. It's the only thing I sleep in all winter."

And just like that, abruptly, without so much as a goodnight, she went to Hubert.

Through the night I shivered alone and groaned in my now-malodorous clothes, wrapped in the robe, bone frozen, nose blue-tipped, my feet despite boots and socks cramping with prehypothermia. Come morning, half-asleep, the loud scrape of chair legs on tile brought me upright. At her big stainless steel desk, she sat typing furiously on a laptop.

"So, you're up," she observed, annoyed.

Rubbing my numbed face, I nodded. "So to speak."

"Sleep was good?" she asked with no real interest.

"I barely slept. It was so cold."

"I thought you were an Israeli soldier once."

"I was."

"Real soldiers don't complain."

"As a matter of fact, they do. And often."

But already I was forgotten in her online search for something which, when found, lit her face with excitement. "Here it is. Listen!"

Multilingual like so many Europeans, she translated aloud into perfect English an interview with her from the morning's edition of a major German daily in which she claimed that Vladimir Putin was not as bad as others made him out but was in fact a real hero poised to defend the West against militant Orientalism—her euphemism for Islam.

"But you can't really believe that," I said, sickened. "He's invading your land. He wants to make it part of Russia again. He's former KGB and it's been proved beyond a shadow of a doubt that he stole the American election even if Trump doesn't seem to give a crap. Russian scandal after Russian scandal is rocking the headlines. Putin controls America!"

"Yes, and I hope he keeps a strong hand on you Progressives. And throws you all into prison. Who else will stand up to the mullahs? Manhattan Millennials? Don't make me laugh. And why do you care about Ukraine? Putin will restore things to how they were before the Soviets fell because Trump will let him. We have entered the Age of the Strongman. Putin will put iron into the flaccid spine of the metrosexual West."

"You're a Ukrainian writer! Don't deny it! You can't defend Putin! You're going to piss off everyone—Germans, Ukrainians, Americans!"

"Don't be hysterical. No. You're wrong. You don't understand lazy people. No one cares. This will only anger Frau Goebbels."

"Frau WHO?"

"My editor. At my German publisher. Typical fanatic Berlin intellectual left-winger and big indignant champion of the Ukrainian underdog. Frau Goebbels hates Putin like poison. She is like you, spineless, and froths at the mouth about socialism and pities the poor immigrants. I call her Frau Goebbels because every word from her homely lips is pure poison New Left propaganda. She reminds me of Ulrike Meinhof, a slogan-spouting idiot ranting about revolution but who would hide under the bed if it actually happened. And why do you think Putin wants to take back Ukraine? He doesn't need more turf. Russia has enough *lebensraum* for three Europes. No, it is because Putin doesn't trust Ukrainians. Do you know what they did to the Jews in World War II? Worse than Nazis! They slaughtered Jews in the public squares of their cities and towns and tortured and massacred them in the death camps. The Ukrainian nationalist anti-Semites want to put the face of Stepan Bandera on their currency."

"I don't know who that is," I said wearily.

"A Cossack dog. When the Germans invaded, Bandera cooperated with them, butchering Jews, and he fought against the Russians on the Nazi side. When Stalin took Ukraine, the KGB shot Bandera as a traitor. But in 2010, Viktor Yushchenko, the Ukrainian president and leader of the anti-Russian nationalists, made Bandera an official state hero. Now there are statues of him, his face on tee shirts and baby bibs, a big pop cult hero, the Ukrainian Che Guevara. This is what Angela Merkel and Frau Goebbels work to support. Only Putin wants to crush these fascistic cockroaches. He alone stands up to PC apologists for Islamic fundamentalist terrorism, the ones like your Negro ex-president Osama Obama."

"Black, not 'Negro,'" I interject bitterly. "And his name is not . . ."

"I know. I know his name. You have a soft mind. Black, Negro, what's the difference? No matter what you call people, they will hate you. Everyone hates Jews. Even me, and I'm Jewish! Look what's going on with American and European colleges. Columbia University. The Sorbonne. Oxford, Berkeley, San Francisco State, the University of Berlin. Jewish students study in fear. Foucault and Derrida have poisoned the well of free thought with their Marxist poststructuralist obsession with colonialism. They, who have colonized Western academia! The Palestinian student organizations are terror cells. Black Lives Matter are shameless little wannabe Maoists. And your Me-Too movements are full of bloodthirsty twenty-first-century Madame Defarges. We hear all about it here in Berlin. How the American mind has been shanghaied by the cult of Self-Pitying Victimization.

"So, yes, I like Putin. And if Trump is Putin's marionette, so what? Trump is an inflatable sex doll from a porno shop. A masturbation aide for the Religious Right. Putin despises him. He has something on him, something bad, very black. Yes, Trump has small hands but look at his hot wife. She hates his guts though. That is what money will buy you. Americans are so interesting. Your beloved ex-president probably has a huge cock. It's why swooning sexually-starved white liberal feminist intellectuals in their dull black cocktail dresses dream of fucking him with their starched pussies, sagging tits, and dry gray pubic hair like steel wool soap pads. To get rid of him, right wing American men elect a white businessman with a tiny penis. Women all over the world know two things absolutely: men with small hands have small dicks and black men have bigger cocks than whites. It is that knowledge that binds us women globally: the true heart of multiculti feminist intersectionality."

"You're going to sink yourself with this kind of crap. You'll lose your publisher. The literary scene will ban you."

"The opposite. I am on the rise. You and all your kind are on the way out. You overthink everything. No instinct. To you, a cigar is Walter Benjamin's cock or Bin Laden's AK-47. Nothing is what it seems. From Adorno and Horkheimer to Marcuse and Derrida, all those dreary anticolonial assholes have colonized your brain. To your colleagues, I am a satirist. The more like this I speak the harder they laugh. I have them rolling in the aisles. I am so off their charts that the Progressives can't imagine that I mean what I say. The more serious I am, the less seriously I am taken. One of them, an important critic, has called me the Ukrainian Vonnegut. What an imbecile! Another compares me to Nietzsche ranting in *The Case of Wagner*. Idiot! When French deconstructionism destroyed the ethical core and the esthetic base, chaos ensued. Moral relativism spread over the whole planet. Every meaningful structure fell, to be replaced by what? Global militant self-pitying entitlement, victimization, and the hedonism of the moral abyss. Through these doors have marched religious fundamentalism, ISIS, Iran, the Christian Right, and all the other poisonous products of a compassless world. And in reaction to which there are idiots, such as you, clinging to your old-world-order values, your humanity, your decency, your Jewish nationalism, and kumbaya progressive piety. The new savages will roll over you like a tank. What I stand for, my alleged amorality, is in fact moral! A subversive commentary. A possible position where none seems to exist."

"You're a nihilist," I spit.

"Tell me, Mr. Morally Nuanced: Why do they hate you? Because you are so sincere! The ridiculous Mister Auschwitz. An oversensitive Zionist shedding molecules of decrepit, outmoded piety, like one sick with the flu. But do you know what? NO ONE GIVES A SHIT ABOUT YOUR HOLOCAUST! Do you know what they say about it? BORING!"

"It's your Holocaust, too. You write articles about it."

"Look at your career. They call you a writer's writer, the polite way of saying that you'll die poor, never win the big prizes. It's a euphemism for 'literary loser.' Why do you wear that stupid tan trench coat? To prove that you are a grave existentialist? The Camus Jew?" She laughed aloud.

"As I recall," I said, "when we met at the festival, I was the headliner on the main stage, appearing before hundreds, while you were a side act in a small lounge playing to an audience of five, who did not laugh once. And if I'm not mistaken your books have yet to be translated into English but several of mine have appeared in German and Dutch as well as British editions. I'm not doing so badly, huh? I don't know what there is to get or what I need to do. I'm tired. I don't agree with the Left or the Right. I don't want to return to Israel or America, although I've received several residency invitations to teach and write. I've declined university teaching posts. They pay poorly and I won't have my course curriculum dictated to me by some white misfit in dreads posing as black.

"I travel. I go. I do my best work in hotel rooms now. The idea came to me from reading about Edvard Munch who painted in one hotel after the next. I like hotels. The sterility. The impermanence. I oversleep, have fatigued adrenals, but in hotel rooms when the heavy brocaded curtains are drawn and the air conditioning hums, it is an eternal, restful twilight. I just want to fuck and write. My career? To hell with it. I think you're jealous of my trench coat. I sense you're a cheapskate but why not go ahead and buy yourself one? Get something in gabardine. You'd look good in gabardine."

"You SHOULD care!" Lena sneered. "The big prizes, the big money, they don't come to the one with no identifiable statement to make. The multiculturalists distrust you. The Right thinks you're soft. Instead of carnival-barking about the Holocaust you should talk about human rights outrages in Indonesia, which, by the way, except for their snake epidemic is a wonderful place for a cheap holiday, if you don't mind finding a twenty-foot python curled in your backyard, with the overweight old-maid next-door neighbor swallowed whole and forming a gigantic bulge in the boa's midsection. It's not so uncommon. The Philippines, where death squads execute drug addicts and drunks in the street, is also a cheap holiday, and the president, Duterte, wants to shoot female rebels in the pussy. The hotels are deluxe places. I love so much the ever-amusing despotic third world. It's what the culturati want to hear about.

"Paint in broad strokes. Make complex statements that no one understands. Mention the UN and The Hague. Go on about injustices—publishers love that shit. Wear your hair in corn rows. Apologize for being a Jewish writer. The Holocaust was too big for goyim to wrap their brains around, even though they committed it. And now everyone hates Israel. Goyim need smaller, more manageable causes like Standing Rock. Be a Water Warrior. Go get stoned in a tent on Native American sacred casino soil, speak in podcasts about the Great Spirit, ball horny phony-blonde squaws from Marin County while tribal leaders run their blackjack tables and call-girl rings. Shed tears on stage in speeches about fracking, Monsanto, the genetic modification of garden seeds! Americans are internationally despised airheads. You should tell everyone that you reject Israel. Be the Vanunu of literature. Many Israeli writers do it. In France no publisher will issue a Hebrew book in translation if it mentions the Israeli Defense Forces in a positive light. The worst critics of Israel in Europe are Israeli writers. Say something good about Israel and you're sunk. Kiss your foreign translation rights good-bye. No invitations to speak at the 92nd Street Y for you. No *New York Times Book Review*. You'll be hated. You should go to France, demand political asylum as a refugee from fascist Zionism, declare yourself an oppressed international writer. When you die, they'll bury you in Père Lachaise Cemetery. Israeli writers will spit on your grave, not in protest but for envy. You could get the Nobel Prize!"

"And you, Lena? You call yourself an international writer?"

"No. I call myself a 'European writer.' Frau Goebbels says that there is no such thing. But I say it in every forum and interview I can. Repeat a lie enough times and it becomes the truth. Trump knows. For years he slept with *Mein Kampf* on his nightstand."

"Fuck it, Lena. You're a Ukrainian Jew who writes in Russian and whose fame rests on the German translations of your books from the biggest publisher in Germany, a country that killed Jews by the millions, including your relatives at Babi Yar. That's not European; that's cultural and historical schizophrenic denial."

"To talk about the Jewish thing in Russia is a professional kiss of death," she said. "In literature, it will finish you off. Also in Ukraine, kaput! In Germany they're sick of gas chambers blah blah. The looks you get from their intelligentsia say, 'Not THAT again!' Besides, what does Treblinka have to do with Snapchat and Instagram? Everyone wants to move on. If someone on Facebook posts something about the death camps, a small handful of old shits used to hit the sad face emoji. But they got rid of that emoji. Now, you can only 'Like' a post. So now what? Hit 'Like' on a photo of corpses in a mass grave? Some do. Anyway, I have nothing to say about Jews. All that Jewish shit kills my heart. I can't relate. I only deal with it when I have to translate some Jewish text for money. Otherwise, when I think of it, I hear a sad fat rabbi groaning in my head: *Oy-vey* this and *Sh'ma* that. Enough already!

"That is why you interested me at the festival. You are like some exotic throwback carnival freak act. A Spotted Leopard Woman with No Arms who knits doilies with her feet. Your prose reeks of chicken fat and pickled illness. You talk about being Jewish like it has meaning to you, like it gives you strength, like anyone out there gives a shit. You proclaim Israel even though your audience boos. You talk Holocaust like it happened to you personally, just yesterday. I first heard you back in Berlin, even before the festival. There's a news film clip from ABC Australia of you at the Edinburgh International Book Festival, alone on stage, facing down an angry audience of BDS-supporting Scots and shrieking Palestinian activists. I thought that you were a satirical performance artist. I told myself that he can't seriously be an Israeli citizen and soldier, having fought in wars, and still believe in all that tired boring old Theodore Herzl-Hemingway crap: this must be performance art. But OMG, you're genuine. You really mean it. Your haunted Jewish piety turns my stomach and yet intrigues me!"

"So, you Googled me?"

The Berlin Woman

"Yes. So what?"

"But on the plane to the festival where I first saw you, you pretended not to notice me."

"On the plane I didn't put you together with the online you. You don't look the same as your black and white publicity photo. In those, you are slim, intelligent, with big dark burning eyes. In real life, you're like a washed-out wrestler with flabby muscles and wearing a stupid stevedore's cap. I thought you were a Macedonian dock worker."

"And I thought you were an Austrian princess."

She glanced away, for a moment, pleased. I asked if Hubert, her husband, will be gone long and when she said that he'd be all day at work, we moved towards each other, embraced, fell onto the cot.

Chapter 2

I wanted gentleness, eagerness, soft lingering kisses. To stroke her cheek, skin, and hair. She felt warm, slender, light.

But when I tried to kiss her, she turned her face and began to fumble with my belt. Then, suddenly, she shoved her groping hand down my pants, clasped my cock, tugged hard; amazed, a little put off, I pushed her hand away. She thrust it back in, fingers like searching tentacles. My cock shrank from her touch. "No," I said, closing my legs like a drunk virgin caught by a masher in the back of a mud-spattered convertible. And again her hand shot down and again I pulled free. At this point my cock crouched trembling in the bushes, trying to make itself as small as possible, to hide. But she thrust her arm around my waist and shoved down and groped as I tried to wriggle free, laughing and yet angry, her small determined hand unstoppable. It struggled down there furiously, like a mongoose battling a snake.

"Why won't you kiss me? Do I have bad breath?" I asked, my voice small, weak, indignant, while thinking, Isn't that exactly what a woman might say?

I pulled her hand away decisively. After all, I was twice her size.

"Why do you turn away your face?" I demanded.

"I don't like to kiss," she said simply.

"How can you not like to kiss? Everyone on earth likes to kiss."

"I don't. It's my right."

"And it's my right to say no when you try to grab my cock."

"You have no rights," she said.

"Look. If this is some S&M power trip, forget it."

"No. I'm no dom. I'm fem. Let's try again. I promise to be good."

So, we tried. But her hand shot down. She let me kiss her

momentarily, then jerked away. She kicked off her panties, pushed me down, scrambled on top, took out my limp shriveled cock, and stuffed it into herself. Resigned, I lay there, let her do as she liked.

During this whole time, I listened for the front door, thought I heard someone, perhaps Hubert. Oblivious to me, Lena hump-grinded against my groin. Somehow my cock slipped in; she was soaking wet down there and my cock hardened as it entered her reluctantly, grew semi-firm, and for a few long minutes we sort of fucked. But there was no love in it. She still would not let me kiss her. I moved away, extricated myself.

"Suck on my tit!" she demanded.

Wearily, I did as commanded.

She began to frig herself furiously. I tried to get into it, gently licked and then firmly sucked on her nipple. Just to get it over with. If she came, I could then regain my feet, for a woman in a mounting orgasmic thrall is a spectacular natural force and holds her partner spellbound. You cannot abandon your post until the storm has passed. To do otherwise is criminal. Though I badly wanted to stand up, I held fast to her. She seemed impervious to the studio's frigid cold. I clasped her other nipple. She moaned.

"Pull on it! Harder!"

I began to stretch it with my mouth, then my fingers. It extended to a length we could have jumped rope with.

"Harder!" she gasped, her buttocks lifting off the bed. "Don't stop!" she whispered. Her hand moved faster and harder, blinding. With a hoarse screech she orgasmed herself.

In a humanitarian gesture I held her protectively, and between us sputtered something like affection. Suddenly, she moved my shirt aside and began to gnaw on my nipple like a child seeking suck. It was strange, unpleasant, not erotic in the least, the working out of some jarring subliminal subconscious urge. I was to mother her like some brood cow. She was effeminizing me. I lay there stiffly, let her do as she liked, my face turned to the window, studying the curtains. It is in such moments that one thinks with a shudder of one's own mother, one's toddlerhood, the shadows, the innocence, the big dark injurious gods. Disgusted, I looked away.

This, I told myself, is how a woman must feel who is quietly being raped.

Chapter 3

Berlin, 2:15 a.m.

Dear Gerhardt,

I write to you from the immense frozen palace of Lena's Kreuzberg flat. Since meeting her I am unable to sleep and seem to have lost all interest in sex. And yet the more unresponsive I become the wetter she grows. She shoves my flaccid meat into her feral cunt, goes romping and riding, a form of corpse-love no doubt, spawned in her native Ukraine where as a kid she lived close by the mass grave at Babi Yar, and her parents drove her each month to some place she described in a flat voice as a grassy unmarked meadow where her father, face expressionless, pointed to a patch of ground and said, "We think your grandfather, three aunts, one uncle, and several distant second cousins are buried somewhere down there." Which she didn't grasp and no one explained. They held the usual tailgate party from the back of their car, sat on folding lawn chairs sunk into the corpse-fertilized grass, feasting on kasha with meatballs, buttered bread, borscht, cucumber salad, and swigs of Orangina. Lena sprawled with legs akimbo jumping up and down and with outspread arms tracing about in a helicopter whirl: wheeeeee! With the sky spinning overhead she fell dizzily to the mass grave laughing.

In the Ukraine a new black market has sprung up. Ernest American Jews inspired by Claude Lanzmann and Steven Spielberg have commissioned small bronze plaques to mark the mass graves where their distant relations perished. In turn, local thieves open them up, excavate the bones, sell them to tourists for souvenirs. Some of these cadaverous relics have started to show up on eBay where you can bid on the femur of a Jewish child. Lena saw one going for nine hundred Ukrainian Hryvnia (about $350 US) and nearly bought it.

"Whatever for?" I smiled unhappily.

"I'm a shopaholic."

For this remark I wanted to leave, never to see her again, but instead stayed, staring at her, spellbound, appalled as she explained—through a mouthful of shawarma in the local Turkish restaurant to which she had dragged me, ravenous from our latest bout of loveless sexual failure—that in Ukraine there is no Seventh Ring of Hell; apparently the rings themselves just keep descending, infinitely, to depraved, unimaginable black depths, each echoing with the unheard cries of murdered Jews. She showed me a website on which people post selfies taken by Millennials yoga-posing downward dogs, Vriksana, and Kapotsana atop the Holocaust memorial in Berlin, and another of a Prague-based modern dance troupe gamboling naked at Auschwitz: a gas chamber Woodstock. Such, she told me, is today's customized and personalized moral core.

In my moral repugnance at myself for engaging in love with her, I cry alone.

Yet, by nature I'm no weeper.

In Dachau I stood tearless before ovens into which picture-snapping tourists tossed their used flashbulbs.

In Frankfurt I bore dry-eyed witness to the cow-tipped gravestones of the Jewish cemetery spray-painted with Swastikas.

Always, I shrugged. What can I do about that? Nothing!

In Lebanon, as a soldier I saw men injured horribly but did not sniffle, not even when Yoav lay there screaming with his foot blown off; not even when Buki, stepping from our position to yawn, stretch, and smile at morning, took one smack in the chest.

I am slowly going nuts, barely have the strength to work. But I promise you, Gerhardt, my friend, swear with a hand on your excellent translation of my book *Kike: A Memoir*, that:

a) I will not kill myself

b) But if I really must then first I will set to words what occurred with Lena so that you and all my friends, acquaintances, colleagues, readers will grasp why I, Nathan Falk, lay me down to die. Having tried so hard without success to explain it to myself, and failed, and needing witness, for my problem after all is that Lena and I are symptomatic of something much larger: we're the self-destructing pawns of a world barreling hell-bent for leather towards Holocaust 2.0 where anti-Semitism like a poison gas seeps in everywhere, on the Left and Right, and all signs point to a resurgence of new improved ghettoes, more streamlined death camps, and greener, more ecologically sound methods of Jew disposal. Today's fascist butchers will be tomorrow's green corpse recyclers.

Who to warn? How? Why even bother? No one cares, or even reads, every single human being almost comatose, face down in a cell phone, soul-stripped, captive to the depraved technological coffin of late-stage capitalism, where cities have turned into a succession of box stores peddling the commodification of Moloch and Baal, and cold-eyed predators like Lena find tired hearts like mine to devour just for the fun of it.

She intuits that I am a writer too broken to produce the dystopic novel for which I have been contracted by Wyndham and Read, the famed publishers. If it ever gets written and published despite Lena, she will, of course, scan it hungrily, not as a colleague but in fear of what her chicken-necked unmanned spouse, Hubert, with his soft sarcastic eyes, effeminized voice, and Eraserhead haircut, might learn not only about our liaison but, even more, about her lover Rolf, and never mind the hundred and one anonymous dicks that she has mounted thanks to chat rooms and social media.

Every place looks like every other place. Even atrocities around the globe seem alike. Keffiyeh-masked killers charge over manicured lawns mowing down tourists. Where? Mumbai? Riyadh? Amman? Tel Aviv? Brussels? Paris? Sleepily, I blink, click, surf—comatose with the uniformity of a globalized world in which any new book is momentarily notable only for its author's name, not its content, and the book cover is just a marketing digital portal, a glyph to open for compulsive purchase of useless dreck.

For if I have learned one thing thanks to the Digital Age it is that content is not just the bait but the trap; we are all cunningly placed to lure each other to a commodified doom, and that absolutely nothing changes anything, neither the hunt nor the capture, the web surf nor the acquisition, the slaughter nor the feast, the campaign nor the election, the lobbying nor the legislation, the scandal nor the scandalized: all transpire in a dizzying parallax of insensate transmission and transaction in a vacuum of perpetual commodity exchange in which nothing, absolutely nothing, is ever consummated, though somewhere far off in some impossibly distant heaven rings the great cash register of the Global Elite, whose machinations produce ever-widening spheres of mass inaction and impotence, so that even sex, fucking, death itself, seem pointless, and *nothing changes anything*. Since meeting Lena that has become my new mantra.

That *nothing* includes motivational speakers, well-intentioned critical thinkers, hip-hoppy political street murals, rap song rages against the machine, leaping and tumbling dance troupes of nubile well-intentioned trust-fund tards with sculpted bods in dance skin, left-wing and liberal editorials, social justice demonstrations, graying pony-tailed socialist philosophers in dirty sneakers holding forth from stages, well-known authors raging at portable mikes from the steps of lionized libraries, artists waging social justice battle with their paint brushes, and journalists gunned down for their corruption scoops.

Nothing, absolutely nothing, deters dictators, blocks violent killers, thwarts graft, reduces gun violence, or even registers as shameless, with some vast compassionate Infinitude profoundly shaken with trembling and tears, bearing hapless and pointless microscopic witness from a tenth-dimensional remove to earth's ceaseless blood orgy of torture, butchery, and mindless mayhem.

Today's shattering news is tomorrow's forgotten headline; everything, good or bad, is just so much grist for brains drunk on digital addiction. "Good" or "evil" notions declared outworn by imbecilic incomprehensible French pedants like Foucault and Derrida have been displaced by contemporary life's only true value markers: How much does it cost? And does it make for good online content?

On these altars do we lay down our own children to perish in the schools, Cineplexes, and malls of demons in trench coats wielding battle-grade assault rifles, or to be abducted, tortured, raped, and decapitated while out jogging by serial-killing late-middle-aged strangers in vans, or to provide fresh meat for lunatic cults performing paroxysmal psychosexual sadomasochistic rituals, or else as child porn captives snatched from home right out of their beds by secret dark pedophilic rings of Internet entrepreneurs.

Lena grasps that the sort of high-minded books I write are simply a throwback, antiquated, a bore, over which I slave, spilling my veins onto every page, though to what end? My books are briefly perused, then placed on the tanks of suburban toilet bowls as pedestals for cinnamon-scented candles from Bed Bath & Beyond, or sold in suburban garage sales along with the pink Fisher-Price Barbie Tough Trike and the Risk Game in the scotch-taped box missing half its pieces.

Of course, she is monstrous, a twisted Berlin-raised Ukrainian Femme Nikita, who deems the former-KGB torturing-colonel Putin to be a kind of messiah. Lena proudly dashes off paeans to the ruthless shirtless horseman that run in heavyweight German and Russian newspapers and periodicals that refer to the Ukrainian city of Lviv as Lemberg (its original name under the Austro-Hungarian empire before it became Lwow as part of the Republic of Poland; but then it changed back, briefly, under the Nazis, to Lemberg, which the Soviets subsequently made Lvov before the Ukrainians settled on Lviv).

Some dismiss Lena's antics as so much avant-garde posturing, a Susan Sontag-style fashionable fascist campiness, a double-helix ironical spoofing of the alt-right. But no. It's real. She can't help herself, is a complete goner, an Alfred Jarry Ubu Roi of mass graves; a futuristic Marinetti caught in a mental shit storm of Holocaust-ravaged genes that, as with me, pretzel-twist her into an agonized historically-disassociated and indefensible posteur bordering on mental illness.

Haven't researchers at the University of Haifa proved that genocidal trauma passed through DNA to the offspring of survivors guarantees to inculcate us with postgenocidal systematic furies? In other words, we of the Second Generation, now known as "2G," were each doomed from birth to suffer intensely and to love each other hopelessly. The Holocaust rules not just our cells but our genitals. When Lena and I helplessly marched into the gas chamber of our love, the only way out was to become skeletal swamis capable of placidly chanting lotus-style on beds of nails. Dressed only in diapers and turbans, faces painted with ash from the Birkenau marshes, we should sit ceaselessly counting to six million and back again.

For it has now been proved that any female whose orifice—mouth, cunt, anus—receives another's sperm forever carries that person's DNA. The perpetually burrowing sperm wiggles deep into the host's brain, spawning quadrillions of replicants until they reach the very seat of thought and motor function where they set up shop, meaning that Lena's mind has not only absconded with her Austrian-born cuckolded husband and the dozens, even hundreds, of avant-garde pan-European one-night-stand psychos that she has rocked between her legs but worse still with the German philosopher Rolf, that Michael Douglas look-alike putz academic with a collapsed six-pack and tennis-bum tan who plugs her every year on three-month-long tropical adultery poverty tours through Africa, India, South America. Her brain is a UN Security Council of alien sperm all conjoined in raging condemnation of me, the outlier American-Israeli. And she has yet another brigade of fuck buddies tucked away throughout Europe—Hungarian museum curators, Flemish private collectors, Italian literary critics, French film directors, Estonian psychiatrists, Serbian dramatists, British choreographers: a compendium of the cultural elite, all of whom to a man or woman, left-wing or right, blindly adore her. With this coterie she Skypes and messages throughout the day in an ongoing ceaseless mutual mass seduction.

Despite knowing that she is perfectly incapable of fidelity, I want to be with her, hold her naked, close to my chest, stroke her stubborn little head, lick her pussy, lie with her, entangled head to toe in a mass-grave 69. And though I know that, even as her fiendish unrelenting mind plots its next pathetic subterfuge, as her loveless cunt clasps my cock like a master sergeant's fist, she will never let me kiss her; inside I perish for love of her, because to be with her spells my own certain and meaningless annihilation.

She is my Final Solution.

Chapter 4

S he loathes earrings.

I bought her a pair, small silver fish, quite lovely.

She held them up, tossed them back into the small ribbon-tied velvet drawstring bag.

"I loathe earrings," she said, pocketing them. I feel sure that later they were sold off or pawned.

How can anyone *loathe* earrings? And yet to me this somehow explains the numbing artificiality of her literary style. For both enlightened Germans and hipster Russians in Picassoesque white and blue striped Russian navy jerseys have zealously decided to enjoy whatever crap earringless Lena writes for the simple reason that she is from Ukraine, a nation invaded by Putin's hated nationalistic militia operatives who waylay Kiev's troops, torture them horribly, and leave their mutilated corpses on the roadside as warning.

Germans worry that Putin intends to retake Russia's old lost eastern bloodlands and ring Western Europe—particularly Germany—with T-14 Armata tanks, Night Hunter helicopters, and the infamous Strategic Rocket Forces armed with super-heavy thermonuclear R-28 Sarmat ICBMs.

But in Berlin, the Ukraine is trending. Though she reviles all things Ukrainian, she stands (rather insistently) among the most noticed in that tiny field of the nation's translation-starved exiles.

We're speaking of a Ukraine in which, according to her, very few even know how to read or write, where poets dwell in threadbare shacks or even chicken coops. She once showed me a Ukrainian hip-hop video in which a young BBW with a face like a shovel and dressed in peasant rags breakdances amid roosters and pigs before a squalid mud hovel while bustin' out rhymes in Ukrainian.

"This is my country," she said. "A rapper in a babushka. Now you understand."

Like her or not, Euro-egghead literati have brainwashed themselves to embrace Lena's acerbic put-downs and even her unfathomable support for Russia's invasion of her homeland.

One night in a Berlin bar, she introduced me reverently to a broad-shouldered pro-Putin Russian brute with long black hair and a broken nose smeared across his acne-scarred face who attained glory by defecating on stages before live audiences while screaming, "This is what I do on Ukraine! Ukraine is mine, bitch!" Evidently audiences of the elite found this incredibly vanguard. I, however, declined to shake his extended feces-laden hand which infuriated Lena.

"You have just refused the hand of genius," she said scornfully.

Curious if he had anything to do with her felonious toilet paper obsession, I later learned that she had fucked the artist and his tattooed Brazilian wife in an excremental threesome, the naked colleagues voiding on each other and shoving unraveled rolls of toilet paper filched from the lavatories of the Berlin National Art Museum up each other's asses—all that caught on video in a film short entitled *Kunst Dreck* that was shown at the 49th Berlin Underground Film Festival to thunderous applause.

No, says my mind, no, you don't love the actual Lena, just some maudlin notion of her, grieving something, someone, that never was, a fantasy.

My heart protests: who is she? Some crazy Eastern European free-lancing thief of hearts, steered by a shirtless, horse-mounted narcissist? An acquisitive Putin in a skirt?

Why am I not grateful this morning, being privileged to lodge in the very finest hotels as a guest of the Northern European Literaturhauses, in which I have always a first-class room with private bath, where I have no need to wipe my hemorrhoidal ass with Lena's rolls of pilfered toilet tissue?

A toilet paper klepto on an unnerving scale, she filches puffy white double-ply rolls handbag-smuggled from the public restrooms of restaurants, cafés, private homes, gala affairs, so that whenever we cohabit, my sitting hunched over a decent crap on a toilet inspires feelings of moral outrage tinged with self-loathing. My ass feels so guilty! By contrast, on this very morning before boarding the train, I had used a legal hotel management-provided roll, and as I wiped, a bracing sense of rectitude puckered my anus—all too short-lived as next I felt struck by a deep gut-wrenching sadness when I spin-flushed my morning deposit down into the excremental deeps of anus mundi: that ass-world inferno of death camps and mass graves, my soul riding Slim Pickens-like astride a Berlin-bound phallic nuke, hoping to penetrate into the mushrooming pit of her disloyal polyamorous post-Brezhnev-era gash, but instead just sitting there, pants huddled around my shoes, weeping, knowing that I would surely see her yet again, though others warn that doing so spells my certain ruin; for she is the predacious dictator of my dick, up for anything; she fancies herself a Russo-German-accented Gogol in Wunderkind land, a surrealistic Turgenev leaping whole from the morgue of post-Soviet identity loss and, consequently, in her weird novels, through which I have skimmed with barely any interest, she undercuts everything and anything like some avenging pernicious Ukrainian Holden Caulfield but sans the kindly Salingeresque wit and despite the fact that with time she has come to physically repulse me; yet once I had succumbed to her will even my protesting cock eventually stood at half-hearted attention to meet her ovarian roll calls, while her husband, Hubert, was away on business or visiting his parents. Yes, I went repeatedly to visit her in Berlin, appalled at myself yet helpless to resist. She literally willed me erect and then fucked me till I dropped and in captivity kept me just barely alive on doll-house-sized bowls of kasha.

When together we ate kasha with eggs. Kasha with sardines. Kasha with sadness. Kasha with noodles. Kasha with fuck. Kasha cunnilingus. Kasha cauliflower. Kasha S&M. Tits and Kasha. And Kasha up the ass.

Lena in bed at 3 a.m., pounding on her tablet, speed-writing a novella entitled "The Kremlin of Kasha," or texting with her Duma of spermatozoic lovers. For Lena, life contains no heroes, only herself. Planet earth is but a mirror in which she sees herself, and all that walks, talks, breathes, calling themselves by name, are but an endless pool of maimed grotesques to exploit and contrast with her own self-proclaimed Lolita-like waifish perfection.

She seems to think mainly about money, the acquisition of flats, and how to further her literary rep.

In her *weltanschauung*, there is no other God but Lena.

Once a week she bathes, then masks her dense minky armpit musk with mid-price perfumes presented to her by those hidden lovers that she ridiculously thinks I don't know of. Wealth is her only ultimate Good, literature little more than a lazy means of social ascent in a Europe tolerant of her brand of rootless, noodling, kasha-flavored Eastern Bloc bohemianism.

Graz

Chapter 5

My book tour for the German-language edition of my memoir *Kike* has gathered enough momentum that I am sustained by the clueless literary salons and ossified cultural institutions of Northern Europe. Well-known as a Jewish second-generation writer of Holocaust-themed novels, the German-speaking lands Austria, Switzerland, Germany welcome me whenever I signal my intention to swing by. I do so often. The money is good. My coffers fill. The children of former Nazis feel edified, absolved.

Interviewed on stages of burnished blond Norwegian wood, I repeat the same thread-worn unctuous phrases and read aloud from the memoir in a hoarse, heartbroken voice that ruptures their haughty faces, brings them to tears, even makes them smile with heartfelt penitence. Here, like a trained circus rider, is their emoting Jew performing on apocalyptic horseback Primo Levian backflips, theosophical Hannah Arendtian handstands, Elie Wieselian somersaults and, for the finale, blindfolded on an aerial Claude Lanzmann trapeze. They soak up all this with somber nods, and their guilty hearts soar with ecstatic remorse.

But lately it has begun to feel that perhaps I have overplayed my hand, lingered long past when I should, hoping that I might yet persuade Lena to marry our fortunes together, even though we are, I feel, fated to lie side by side, naked adulterers, with well-deserved bullets in our remorseless skulls and mass grave dirt in our mouths.

I am already so far past the publisher's deadline for my next book, "Masada X," that the in-house editor assigned to the proposed book no longer takes my rambling calls. An email was even sent from Wyndham and Read's legal department to my agent, Shimone, hinting of possible legal repercussions unless I produce the contracted-for full-length manuscript. It is the one time that Shimone completely lost it with me, shrieking into the phone, "GODDAMN YOU, FALK! Have you lost your fucking mind? You're blowing the best shot you or I have ever had. Whatever you're doing, whoever that stupid Polish cunt is . . ."

"She's Ukrainian"

"I DON'T GIVE A FUCK IF SHE'S TONY SOPRANO'S ONE-LEGGED GOOMAH! STOP IT NOW! WRITE THAT FUCKING BOOK!" hanging up before I could promise to do what, in my heart, I knew I couldn't.

Instead of writing, I slept, tossed and turned, and dreamed that a stroke had withered my right hand, my writing hand, into a kind of flipper; that I swam in a sea of strange fish all with Hitler moustaches. The fish seemed to know me, for the moment I appeared they rushed me with wild looks in their fishy eyes. I woke with a start, realized that I yet had all five fingers, was now in a hotel room in Graz, Austria, on book tour.

If only, I thought, I could just start the next novel, the one for which I've been contracted in a six-figure deal cinched by the frenetic Shimone. Israeli-born, not one of the best in the business, he had pulled all of his inconsiderable weight to score big; announced the deal to me screaming over the phone long distance from New York, through a mouthful of lox on pumpernickel bagel. It was for a lot, a quarter mil. Fifteen percent to him, the rest to me, one-third on signing, one-third on manuscript delivery, one-third on publication.

"The book will make us zillionaires!" he howled. "We'll fuck strippers, drop Quaaludes, live like the Wolf of Wall Street! They'll make a movie of it with Brad Pitt and Eric Bana. Both. You'll see!" And in fact, his film agent was chafing at the bit to see the finished book.

Shimone had performed an unheard-of feat: sold the book rights while managing to retain the film rights; said in all serious-ness that during one conversation with the film agent, Ridley Scott had tossed out a possible two-million-dollar figure. With that, Shimone could finally put money down on that McMansion in Herzliya he spoke constantly about. An even bigger miracle: his wife, Mitzi, a former Victoria Secrets model, even said that if a film happens she'll have me out to their home for lunch—an unheard of promise, given that Shimone regards all the male writers in his stable as sociopaths out to fuck his wife, which is not far from the truth; he guards her like a Doberman.

The futuristic book's protagonist, Meir Hadlai, is a celebrated but dissipated twenty-second-century bed-hopping former Israeli war hero and washed out Special Forces captain from Sayeret Matkal, now drinking himself into oblivion and embroiled in degrading affairs with hot young women or wanton wives who use him as a boy toy, then toss him aside when done. Around him the entire world, including Israel's American allies, has turned against the Jewish state. Israel is collapsing under an apocalyptic Warsaw Ghetto-like resistance against the invading hordes of an international confederation of homicidal anti-Semites. The Israelis, despite their heroic stand, cannot hold out, and in one last desperate stab turn to Meir to lead the last Tavor-toting remnants (think *Mad Max* in Hebrew).

Just the thought of laying down a single line of this preposterous project, born from my own twisted brain, deflates me into a state of baffled impotence.

What possible impact could a novel have upon the real and present global war against the Jews, one waged not only with AK-47s, homicidal vehicles, suicide bombs, and kitchen butcher knives, but Facebook "Likes" and emojis and YouTube jihadi sermons?

On one such Facebook page a Salafist cell dedicated to the "Caliphate" and calling itself the Revolutionary Islamic Brotherhood has begun to post the faces, names, and addresses of prominent Jews, with a call to all Mohammedans to find and kill "The Zionist Defilers" of which, evidently, I am one. My own face is posted there with an old long-defunct Jerusalem address.

When Jews tried to persuade Facebook to remove the page, Facebook replied that nothing about it violates policy: it would remain.

When I reported another page entitled "Jewish Ritual Human Sacrifice of Gentiles" as anti-Semitic, Facebook replied that the page did not transgress their community standards.

In the meantime, the world jockeys to preserve a worthless nuclear pact with Iran; Hamas is tunneling to its next war; Hezbollah, with cash supplied by Iran, has stockpiled a hundred thousand missiles aimed at Israel; and there is ISIS, which, though declared as defeated is still crucifying Christian Arab children, beheading civilians, pitching gays from roofs, and kidnapping Yazidi women for slave-market use in torture sex games.

I want to sleep and then sleep some more, for when drifting into blessed sleep with my depressed head hidden under hotel covers, I can safely attempt to decode the meaning of recent events that prefigure the nightmare I have been contracted to portray.

For, all along, it's been revealing itself in stages, unfolding in bloodier and bloodier clues.

There were the hijackings, the bus bombings, the murder of poor Ilan Halimi, a Parisian Jewish boy kidnapped by a gang of Arab teenagers from the slums, tortured nonstop for weeks, and then slain.

There was the French Salafist in motorcycle gear who put his gun to the brow of a nine-year-old girl named Miriam in a Jewish day school in Toulouse and, when it jammed, cleared the jam, returned the gun barrel to her trembling face, and blew her brains out. He then gunned down her classmate and her rabbi-teacher.

There was the hit man in Brussels who mowed down Jews in a museum with an assault rifle and got away, only to reappear in Syria, gloating and boasting via webcam.

There were armed terrorists in Paris's Marais Jewish quarter, blasting Jewish customers in a Kosher butcher shop; a rabbi stomped to death by thugs in Berlin; in Britain, a synagogue stormed by an angry mob of BDSers; in Israel, Jews run over by drivers who exited their vehicles swinging axes to chop their injured and stunned victims to pieces.

A sense that we are universally targeted pervades my ether. Something must be done! But since when has a novel ever stopped an anti-Semite's crowbar from cleaving a Jewish skull? My heart sinks. The words die.

All along, the mounting horror was there, clear; we just refused to see it. Still do. All along, groundwork has been laid for Holocaust 2.0.

Even as early as when my survivor-mother had first uttered the word "Auschwitz" to me, while others grew up confident of the future, that "Never Again" meant just that, I felt an inexplicable certainty of impending doom—an impossible-to-prove intimation that a second catastrophe was not only certain but imminent.

Lena is somehow an unwitting sexualized prosopopoeia of my worst fears, an oracular avatar of all that will soon destroy us; who senses, I think, that she will count among its first and prettiest victims: an undressed doll dropped dead into a mass grave.

Hence, the fatal drive behind her emotionally suicidal sexual, esthetic, and political brutality.

I had not thought it would come as it has; I wrongly imagined that it would only wear a keffiyeh, but it appears in many guises: faces wrapped in scarves, hoodie-shrouded buzz-cut men Seig Heiling, the bare-chested iron-fisted premier-for-life on a cantering horse; or a bloated Mussolini-like blimp with blond hair and tiny hands; all these bode a single outcome—the mass destruction of my people.

This is the hallucinatory gestalt that shook me when Lena showed me the history book photo of her stripped relations shivering on the edge of the murder pit, including the aunt of whom Lena is the spitting image. For here, in Lena, the very Dead have arisen, sent a message: to love me, destroy me. Here was my poison Eve to rend me rib from cage, tear revelation from my sinew as torrents of aborted prose.

I felt as Theodor Herzl, the father of modern Zionism, might have in Paris when shocked by the lurid public degradation of Alfred Dreyfus before a horde of rabidly anti-Semitic Frenchman screeching *Sale Juif!* "Dirty Jew!" at that absurd and yet touchingly loyal assimilated Jewish career army captain, who stood falsely accused of treason, stripped of his rank, publicly slapped, then shipped off to die in the penal colony of Devil's Island.

Herzl rushed home, agitated, to pace his Paris flat, consider what he had just seen; he had a kind of nervous breakdown during which he first concluded that the Jews must convert to Christianity, an end be made for once and all of Judaism, but then decided that, no, conversion would never work. How could it? But what then will?

He ponders and scribbles and thinks and paces. Feverish, he jumps down to his desk and in five sleepless days and nights of marathon composition pours himself into a brilliant pamphlet-length tract entitled "The Jewish State," which leads, fifty years later, after the murder of six million Jews, to the birth of the State of Israel.

Now there is a Jewish state, yet somehow we remain doomed. In the age of Facebook, no inspired pamphlet can stay the hatred, grotesque and lethal, whose inexorable avalanche threatens to grind our very bones to dust.

In the end, this was my proposal to the publisher, to write a futuristic dystopic *roman à clef* such as no one had ever before seen which would conjure a postmodern world mobilizing for Judeocide.

It would be a novel that I felt sure would inspire ferocious global debate. There would be lectures. Articles. Panel discussions. Book signings. Televised appearances.

I burned with the prospect of the countless invitations to speaking engagements and panels that would pour in until, eventually, I would bring the subject of anti-Semitism before the very United Nations itself, even the EU, perhaps even a special American congressional hearing.

Slowly, with a dignified look of Herzlian gravitas I would mount the podium, deliver stirring testimony.

Afire with this notion, having convinced even the begrudging Shimone to expend his only good contacts to pitch it, my vision won. On the strength alone of a three-page proposal, without even a sample chapter or so much as an outline to show, the book was signed, and the advance was a small fortune. For a time I even considered growing a prophetic hipster beard.

Whereupon, suddenly, I met Lena, my dybbuk, who drained me of all sense of purpose, all will to act, so that I no longer want to prevent mass murder. I just want her to give me a good blow job.

Salzburg

Chapter 6

Passing through the Swiss Alps, with small white-walled and red-shingled chalets arrayed along a lake the blue color of a high-priced call girl's eyes, I am bored.

Other passengers aboard the high-speed ICN tilting train stare out their windows transfixed, jump up to aim black cameras with thick-barreled lenses like antitank missile launchers. But to me, the whole spectacle of rocks, snow, lakes, chalets, and cheesy sky makes me want to puke.

Schroeder, my publisher, is away in France. On his return we'll rendezvous in Salzburg, a tourist town, where he will let me know into what hotel I am booked and where to meet Gerhardt before the evening's event. In the Literaturhaus Gerhardt will read from his translation of my memoir *Kike*, then interview me on stage.

Afterward, I'll sit like a putz, autographing copies of the book.

Were it not for Gerhardt none of this would have occurred. Gerhardt, who is Austrian, from the culturally-despised region of the Tyrol, arranged for my book's publication, even set up the tour. Until recently, he had been a big star of Lena's publisher, Kornbuch Verlag. In fact, with ten critically-acclaimed novels already behind him—including the classic *bildungsroman*, *The Village* (a book hailed by critics as the *Buddenbrooks* of Austria), in which a shy, brilliant, socially inept, and neurotically masturbating boy grows up in a small Tyrolean hamlet among fervid drunken anti-Semitic former Nazis and suicidal, sexually-addicted ski instructors (including his father and four brothers, who all bear a close resemblance to the Brothers Karamazov)—Gerhardt had been Kornbuch Verlag's surest shot for a Nobel.

But his eleventh novel nearly sank him. With this book he came close to complete expulsion from the German literary set. He had been like a son to Victor Olsen, the snowy-haired founder of Kornbuch. A doddering old fellow, Olsen, in one last grab for happiness, had married a bizarre, though beautiful, practicing White Witch. On Olsen's death, she obtained by means of potent legal sorcery, rule over the entire Kornbuch publishing empire and proceeded to bury alive most of Olsen's favorite authors—particularly Gerhardt whom she loathed as a rival for his loyalty— and to promote, instead, chiefly writers of declared New Age proclivities.

It was a bid for the subnormal kitchen-set fans of Oprah and other mesmerized minions of daytime television talk shows, especially those showcases for hucksters offering evangelical soap opera hope to Germany's own version of America's sexless and penniless diet fad and pop spirituality-sickened overweight masses whose kids are off spiking methamphetamine and whose husbands are having liaisons with permed twenty-year-old cashiers from Aldi discount stores. The widow Olsen's aim was to saturate the German-speaking world with pastel-colored books about Gratitude as Practice and Living in The Now.

Gerhardt did a wonderfully Maileresque and quite self-destructive thing: he wrote a scathing novel satirizing the Kornbuch marital takeover in which the witch wife murders her aging spouse, gets away with it, and obtains control of his assets by means of obscene midnight masses involving vomitous potions and orgiastic satanic anal impregnations and dildoing Albanian rent boys from the streets of Schoeneberg, Berlin. As Gerhardt explained to me in detail, in his novel during one of these rituals a rent boy is human-sacrificed by Olsen's widow, his heart torn from his chest and devoured. I still can't shake from my thoughts the image of her Cover Girl face spattered with blood, bits of heart meat stuck to her teeth. But in the book's harrowing finale, she first flosses, then dumps the boy's plastic-wrapped corpse into the River Havel, which flows from north to south through West Berlin, and drives off to appear in an onstage interview at the prestigious literary venue, The Literarisches Colloquium Berlin, where she tips wine glasses onstage with the former Nobel

Prize-winner Günther Grass, author of *The Tin Drum* and an admitted former Nazi.

What made Gerhardt self-destruct? Norman Mailer taught that now and then writers must destroy their whole career from the bottom up: remake yourself from scratch or risk losing your gift. Joyce knew it. So did Cormac McCarthy. But if only Hemingway had done so! Faulkner too. Both died drunks. Now was Gerhardt's turn. He had ten books and a booming rep. The moment had come to blast it all to hell. Certain discerning critics grasped his tactic in the new book, showered favor. Most of the imbecilic and fawning loyalists lined up behind the widow-sorceress to hunt down Gerhardt's head for their critical stew pots.

At first, Gerhardt absorbed the shock of widespread disapproval with aplomb. However, he is the furthest thing from confident that one can possibly imagine. He may come off as self-assured at first but soon the uncertainty shows through; he starts out looking like James Mason and ends up resembling Kafka at the family dinner table. I have met the red-faced lederhosen-wearing wild men of the Alps, who have the stubbornness of lustful rams, a willingness to crush all in their path for the gratification of whatever drunken spontaneous urge provokes their famished limbic systems. That is not Gerhardt who, in matters involving others, is a born gentleman, an elegant former physicist, and nearly always a diplomatic social tactician of the first rank.

This confirmed intellectual has nothing to prove and, of course, as regards the ladies he has often found himself overwhelmed by scores of attractive females. But the tsunami of opposition to his new book was devastating. Quickly, he realized that tact and good manners won't help you in a war. All you can do is save your ass. Somehow, Gerhardt succeeded in doing just that, though exactly how is hard to say. He jumped ship for another publisher, one nearly as powerful as Kornbuch (though not quite).

Of course, at this new house he was no one special—just a mid-career rising name, a good earner, to be used up as best they

ALAN KAUFMAN

could until every *pfennig* had been squeezed from his critically-acclaimed veins.

They sent him off on a grueling, emotionally-crippling nonstop tour not only through Germany and Austria but Paris, Rome, Warsaw, Prague, Budapest, Madrid, and even to London where two of his novels appeared simultaneously in English translation; but none of the many translations of his work fared well. He sold a few hundred in each land. No matter. He traveled, city to city, nation to nation, always one step ahead of the horrible scandal brewing over his notorious book, and the Kornbuch critical assassins dogged his heels, like outraged Maltese knights pursuing Caravaggio who, effectively, had told them to shove their swords and crosses up their unctuous asses.

Chapter 7

In my room in the Hotel Mozart I flipped up the laptop screen, logged onto Skype. Next to her name and face in my displayed list of contacts a green luminous dot indicated that Lena was available. Should I call?

It was early still. Her husband might be up. I wanted to but didn't. Looking at her face felt like ingesting a powerfully addictive opiate. Rushes of ecstatic feeling lifted me higher and higher. She ascends into light; I am trailing behind like a vapor, love-leashed to the tip of her outstretched finger. A Lilith slowly murdering me with frenetic ecstatic unhappiness, her blood my clot, her cells my jails, her breath my death, as though to show to me the fatal inescapable dictum that punctuates our every living act: "In the end you are alone, and you shall die!" She and I slaughter each other just by being alive. If she should die I would too, since she respires me . . . Lena, if you knew, understood (and I believe that you do but must pretend not to) how I need to smoke your hair, sip your dear cheek with my hand, lean my ghost close to your face, breathe your voice, watch your every movement's celestial locomotion among astral planes twinkling in the multiverse of your treacherous body.

I slammed the laptop shut. I sat at the hotel desk with a small lamp on, the rest of the room in darkness, my hand resting on a hotel stationary pad on which, I felt sure, it would be best to leave the last note that I would write to her before my mortal exit . . . Fishing out my cock, after a bare few strokes, I spattered her Skype profile face with a jet of still-warm cum, then lie there spent, thinking that I need to shove Lena from my thoughts, but how?

When in her presence or on Skype, like a gaping boy I sit watchful, adoring; some inexplicable mesmerizing quality reminds me of the smart young middle-class girls that I craved in my urchin youth; the ones whose math tests I cheated off of, whose homework I cribbed, those chubby pink thighs I sometimes slid my hand along, a tarantula inching toward joys concealed by flower-patterned cotton undies.

To a point, the girls pityingly allowed my unrewarded lusty lurking but spoke to me as one would to an escaped zoo beast. For in many ways I was just that: good-looking, rough-hewn, sturdy, with curly black hair, mischievous eyes, dimpled apple cheeks, a rag-clothed guttersnipe tramping about in a hanged man's shoes, always hungry, reeking of railroad soot and arson, teeth unbrushed, and with dirt-scooped ears and armadillo fingernails. I had butt smell.

Teachers were always sending me home with notes about my "deplorable hygiene," which my mother, Myriam, a French-Jewish Holocaust survivor whose own hygiene was deplorable, tore up. She wouldn't let me use deodorant or even toothpaste to brush my teeth. She tapped ashes from her cigarette into the claw of my small hand. "Use that," she ordered. "In the camp, we brushed with ashes. And not from cigarettes either!" Meaning, I guess, the human ashes belched from the crematoria that snowed all over the deathcamp pajama scarecrows.

There was never enough food. She sent me out the door each day on bread shredded into a bowl of powdered milk, the whole buried under a mound of white sugar. This was to last me until supper's fried potatoes served up piping hot with canned cream corn—the thought of which, even now, causes me involuntarily to retch.

I never got invited to the nice girls' make-out shindigs, never got past the inner thigh, to cop a feel under their starter bras all the way past their panties or just to do it, go "all the way" on a sofa. Never made out by a red light bulb to the stoned laments of the Beatles in *The White Album*, playing their subliminal Mansonesque helter-skelter messages to our pubescent brains. What pleasures these pubertal girls allowed me were offered in stairwells, behind walls, on rooftops, or shivering at twilight in parks, always out of sight of others, as though I were some shameful hobo child, used to a point and tossed away. But though there was cruelty, even contempt, in their damp panty offerings, still, it was sweetly exploitive, driven by innocent shame and blind hunger.

But now there is Lena, in so many ways like those girls from decent homes whom I loved in youth, yet utterly indecent, monstrous, demonic, holding me witch-like, spellbound to the old dream of Beatles-smooching on parental sofas, that smell of Lemon Pledge and Mom, yet withholding her red-lipsticked pliable Satanic mouth, offering the jealous torments of her democratically insatiable cunt but refusing the intimacy of my kisses.

Chapter 8

ISkype Schroeder. Beefy and sweaty, my publisher lumbers onscreen, plops down in a chair with an arthritic groan. Huge, red-faced, sweating, wearing his usual empathetic smile in which lurks the cold-blooded amusement of a soulless bureaucrat, Schroeder, before embarking on a career in books, served for over twenty years in the Insurance Division of the Austrian Civil Service where he learned to operate by a single sacred tenet that he has sought in all ways to uphold: "Not My Fucking Department!" This sweeping personal Executive Privileges Act entitles him to blow off all appeals for sympathy, help, rescue, love, and so on.

Of course, he knows all about Lena.

"Falk," he laughs. "Don't look so sad. It's okay."

"Lena has me by the throat."

"I warned you. But you ignore your publisher, who loves you. Now: it is Not My Fucking Department."

"Wrong. It's your department because if I off myself tonight in this hotel, which I'm thinking seriously of doing, the scandal will ruin you and your crappy little scrappy publishing firm."

"To the contrary, Falk. In fact, I wish you would do it. Your death will make a terrible stink. Author suicides sell books."

"You're a bastard, Schroeder."

"I know it. A very big one."

"But I love you. I feel better to see your ugly red face."

"And I you. At the festival I tried to warn you about her. She's insane."

"To hell with her. How are sales so far?"

He grimaced.

"Reviews?"

"All raves. But no one cares."

"What do they say?"

"The best ones compared you to Philip Roth but said you have a bigger nut sack."

"Roth! He was a middle-class shmuck with walnuts for balls. Michael Chabon is his Judaism and Israel-hating Mini-Me. I call them Shtick and Schmaltz. Roth, Shtick; Chabon, Schmaltz.

While Chabon lay what miniscule talent he had on the Moloch altar of Hollywood, Roth, to his credit, finally had ceased to write the same book over and over: that is, he stopped writing altogether—announced, nobly, with touching gravitas, the laying down of his blunted pen-sword, a kind of self-castration, bidding good-bye to Lit as his burning funeral ship sailed slowly over the waterfalls.

No one waved aloha; there were no outcries of grief, but only a brief flurry of the sort of appreciative critical commentary usually reserved for the recently departed and which appeared in the usual Rhino-cardigan-set print graveyards: *The New York Review of Books, The New Yorker, The New York Times Book Review, The Paris Review, The Times of London, Commentary*—all Roth's standard haunts.

One might think it a grand club to belong to, after all, until one considers that one must unto death commingle with the same bland sweater-rack habitués from Barney's, Bergdorf, and Paul Stuart, inhaling the same rank fetor of New York steak, whiskey, flatulence, and Mennen's off the ruddy jowls and shoulders of the same platinum-coiffed self-inflated windbag rhinos and bores. Then, then, and only then does one rush screaming from one's own life, as Roth did, though with the panic well concealed behind a five o'clock shadow, eyes bandit-masked with racoon rings of insomniac literary self-abnegation.

Though he declared quits, somehow Roth lived on in a kind of Twilight Zone, and there was something truly dreadful about that, as though a career ghost still limped among us, a spirit of Pulitzer's past, witness to his own inexorable slide into timeless irrelevance. For already, a new beer-chugging, Klonopin-popping generation of MFA aspirants now crowd literature's hallowed vestibules, and they could care less about Philip Roth.

The youthful outlaw sensation of *Portnoy's Complaint and Goodbye, Columbus* became the Nixon-era Noxzema-reeking dead white male, haunting his own expired Hamletian early success. In Roth's version of the Bard's play, the tormented Danish prince dies unremarked—while the Dad King's ghost soldiers on, dethroned, unalive, but still nudging neighboring Stockholm for a Nobel.

"Schroeder," I yawned at the Skype screen. "We're gonna meet or what?"

"Give me half an hour to slap on some cologne and make myself pretty. I'll come to your hotel."

Thirty minutes later Schroeder waded through the door, immense and beaming with his slightly myopic blue eyes behind gold-rimmed aviator-frame glasses—a great smile of a man dedicated to publishing the translated work of literary renegades.

"Schroeder," I laughed. We embraced. I loved the guy, insofar as I was capable of feeling anything for anyone but Lena who owned my very thoughts.

"You crazy sonofabitch. I missed you! What have you let this stupid woman do to you? You look like shit! We must go meet Edwin. He's a friend. He will cure you. Gerhardt will meet us later at the Literaturhaus Salzberg. An article about you has appeared in this morning's *Der Standard*, Austria's most important paper. Of course, by tomorrow they'll forget you. Austrians have selective attention spans. The only famous people they continue to worship are the von Trapps."

"Fuck the von Trapps. I'm bigger."

"You wouldn't want to fuck them. The only ones left are decrepit old shits. I told you, my ex-wife knew them, yes? Millionaires! So, we go now. Edwin will meet us in a café. It's a nice walk. Come."

"Just give me a minute. I'll meet you in the lobby."

Everyone in Austria claims to have personally known the von Trapps, the heroic anti-Nazi singing family of the film musical *The Sound of Music*, as though association with them absolves one of all connections to the Nazis and expunges all connection to the

Holocaust. But of course, while almost all Austrians were Nazi supporters and in some way or another contributed to the annihilation of the Jews, few living Austrians actually knew the von Trapps or knew someone who did. During the Anschluss, when Hitler marched into Austria, nearly everyone's older relations who were alive in the war had certainly Seig Heiled der Führer, eyes beaming. Probably, Schroeder's paterfamilias had laughed himself sick as Jews on hands and knees scrubbed Vienna's venerable cobblestones; grinned back charmingly in the SS public relations snapshots. Later, in Operation Barbarossa, Papa Schroeder invaded Russia, burning and killing everyone and everything. This is what they all did without exception. How many Jews were on Poppa's head, Schroeder, the son, had no wish to know.

But to me, it made no sense to remain willfully ignorant of war crimes that one's own father must have committed. Of course, there are things that one can't bear to know. And yet, it is my firm belief that those are the very things that we must try to face. But I am too bored to plague anyone, Austrians and Germans included, with this philosophical horseshit. Imagine the unremarked horrors occurring each day: the Syrian child nailed by masked ISIS fanatics to a makeshift cross, his screaming face posted on Facebook for the length of a few angry emojis before the hive-mind's fickle attention span moves on. Thanks to social media we have lost life's last comfort: the anonymity of communal indifference to atrocity.

Everyone these days is determined to YouTube reality at all costs. Why not Schroeder too? Or perhaps he already knows, has found out, prefers not to say. It might be the cause of his chronic smiling. After all, how would one get up in the morning once one admits to oneself all there is to know about everything? Buried deep down, Schroeder must know, but only a little of it seeps bubbling upwards like gas released from decomposing corpses in mass graves. His cold jelly smile defends against this, a form of sleep. Just as Lena is the source of my constant need for sleep. Certainly, she is the cause of my falling. I had Skyped her.

"I have a question."

"Yes, darling."

"Are you really going to Cuba with him?"

"Yes," she said; she'd be stopping in Cuba en route to Panama, a big dream of hers, to see the sun-beaten pastel colors there. Which made me think of her perennial adulterous lover, Rolf, as some kind of Brando-like Stanley Kowalski making her see "the colored lights" in some paint-peeling sclerotic-blue Havana bedroom with a rust-eaten balcony; and as she spoke, voice fading, her face registered my on-screen anguish. I fell so far down into the abyss of the unwritten book rotting inside my soul that I entirely dissociated, left my body, as I moaned aloud at her Skyped face, feeling like an umbilically-strangled fetus.

Almost angrily, she demanded, "Why hurt? Grow up! What else do you expect me to do? The ticket is bought and paid for. No refund is available. What choice do I have but to go?" And then: "Be practical! Stop judging and start living! You should know better. You're too experienced to get jealous!"

I let her go on like that for a while, thinking of how she had no choice but to fuck him, as she does each year, for three months in beach cabins along the Caribbean, all for the price of an airplane ticket. Her voice grew somber, more distinct. She began to hammer at me about my unlaundered wardrobe, the way I eat, my dirty unclipped fingernails, my poor hygiene, my nomadic lifestyle of constant travel by train or plane from hotel to bookstore to Literaturhaus to university. In this respect, she is right. I dread to stop moving. Willingly I absorbed her verbal savaging until the pain was so great that I clamped my teeth into a lifeless, apprehensive smile, afraid to blurt out something that I would later regret.

"I have to go. Schroeder is waiting."

She sighed. "Okay. Whatever. Go."

"Can I try to call you later?" I asked quickly, panicked, like an abandoned infant.

"Uh, SMS first, please. In case Hubert comes." Poor bastard.

Chapter 9

We head out into the boulevards of Salzburg, a regal town of Ancien Régime decadence teeming with rich ogresses costumed in the fashion of the season: chiffon pastel-colored short-shorts and brief Lululemon yoga tops showing lots of belly, patent leather stiletto high heels, and oversized yachting Ray-Bans. Many wear severe ponytails and have wrinkle-free tan and perfect skin pampered in costly alpine dermatalogical clinics where Chinese women attired in thrift shop moo moos pack their faces in mud and massage their varicosities.

Seated out under awnings they suck at straws stabbed into tall soda glasses and puff asthmatically on long slender hand-crafted cigarillos, while constantly swiveling and scanning to see who looks their way, or else who is strolling down the gilded avenues trailing long perfumy trains of oceanic wealth.

The men are toads.

Squadrons of tourist couples, vulgar, in Bermuda shorts and big safari sun hats, the women indistinguishable from their men, only smaller, loudly glom onto anything Mozartian, gripped with Mozart fever, as Salzburg had been the final residence of Wolfgang Amadeus Mozart. His countenance appears everywhere, as once did Hitler's face, on chocolates and soaps, hotel walls, ads for clothiers, restaurant windows, tee shirts, and even printed onto handbags. Mozart's image has become a swastika of postwar Salzburgian affluence, though Mozart himself, a pauper at death, was tossed by city officials into an anonymous mass grave, as later murdered Jews were steam shoveled en masse, though of course Mozart was at least dead when thrown in—not murdered, just broke. Jews were not so lucky.

In a fitting revenge for this dismissive indignity visited upon the great composer, the whole city has become one big festive Mozart crypt, so to speak, and Mozart himself transformed into a bewigged Orwellian Big Brother symbol plastered across every available inch of public wall space. As we come to the appointed café, a sprawl of tables, sun umbrellas, and rather seedy clientele—some of whom are, I'm sure, members of the local Serbian underworld—we seat ourselves, and Schroeder orders for me a double espresso, as I don't drink booze, and for himself a tall sweating stein of ice-cold beer. Both cup and stein come bearing the image of Wolfgang Amadeus.

"At the festival, I saw—and in fact everyone but you saw—that you are in love with a lunatic. It is plain that what Lena feels for you is bullshit. But you are too emotional to see it. This is a woman who cheats on her husband, is known to be disturbed. What good for you could possibly come from such a liaison? Now tell your Uncle Schroeder, do you understand that she will destroy you and what exactly the fuck is happening?"

"At the festival, nothing happened."

"Why do you lie to your publisher?"

"I swear . . ."

"Go on." He sipped from the stein, wiped his lips with the back of his hand. "Tell me the whole sordid shit."

"Just once, we went to lunch. That's all. Look, none of this makes sense. It started in the airport in Vienna, on the nearly empty flight to Innsbruck. Here she comes down the aisle and I could hardly believe my eyes. She sits down across from me even though there's a million available seats. I'd never seen a more beautiful woman in my life. I couldn't believe my good luck."

"Like finding a tumor and thinking you've won the lottery. Yes, she is beautiful. But she is evil. Look at your face! What she's done to you! The review this morning in the paper gives me hope that the translation of your book will make us both rich. Do you know what kind of beautiful women will lift their skirts to you if things work out? Tyrolean fashion models. Swiss ballet dancers. Not peasant dirt from Lviv. Forget about her! We just need a few more raves in the big Berlin papers. And I told you, I'm still waiting on *Der Spiegel*."

"So, how much money are you putting into the book's promotion?"

"Asshole," he smiled. "Do you know how much I have already spent on you and your worthless book?"

"I told you when you contracted me for it: I'll sink you. Look, Schroeder, about Lena—can you please try to understand—I don't want to feel alienated from you. I'm in love. It's serious. More than you know. I don't understand why. I feel like I'm in free fall. On the plane I felt choked and awkward. Like a kid. Wanted to strike up a conversation but couldn't. The whole way to Innsbruck she sat and wrote on her tablet, never once looked at me."

"That should have told you something."

"It told me that she is an aristocrat. Some kind of Austrian princess."

Schroeder stared at me.

"I know what you're thinking . . ." I said.

"No, you don't. I'm thinking that you really have a five-year-old mind. Honestly, I never knew. Can you please tell me how writing on a tablet and not picking up one's head to look at you equals royal blue blood in her? First, most Austrian princesses are inbred mental defectives. And second, she's a Ukrainian. You know about them, yes? Them and the Russians. How they are utterly ruthless, heartless, beasts in human disguise."

"And you sound like Admiral Jodl giving the last briefing before the attack on Stalingrad. What do you have against her? Listen, it was fated, okay? When we landed in Innsbruck, I rushed off the plane. I ran, I swear, as fast as I could to get to my luggage and forget all about her. But I couldn't forget. My heart beat insanely. I looked around for her, searching. When she passed by, luggage in hand, she glanced just once at me, but in that moment, I lived and died in a lifetime. Then, she was gone. That should have been the end of it. But I knew that, though I'd never see her again, I'd love her forever."

"What the hell is wrong with you? What are you talking about? You sound like a cheap romance novel."

"I knew it was fated. That's what I'm talking about. Not a choice. A destiny. When I stepped from the terminal there was Rudy with the festival car, and there she was right next to him. He held up a sign with two names on it: mine and hers. That's when I knew that the gods were in on this."

"Just like a schoolboy! This is very embarrassing. As great a writer as you are, you have the maturity of a duck. You and I both know that, at heart, when it comes to love, you're shit. How many girlfriends have you had? And a few wives, no? Perhaps all geniuses are stupid that way. When you were growing up didn't someone tell you that the names on a handwritten sign held up by a chauffeur are not an invitation to commit adultery? Do you think that you can just carry on like this without experiencing consequences? Take my word for it, she is going to kill you. Rudy said that you were hitting on her as soon as you were seated in the car. So, don't talk crap to me about fate. You chose her. You're choosing, not some gods."

I nodded. "At that point, let's just say that from the moment I saw her I was determined, so, of course, yes, you're right. It wouldn't have mattered."

"There is a husband in Berlin, right?"

I looked down at my hands. Nodded.

"You've met this husband. You told me you even liked him. But how do you think he felt having you around banging his wife while he was at work? It's wrong! You can't go ahead with this. She will never leave him. Look at your face. It hurts to see. You're not yourself. You're not anything. It's like voodoo. You look like a real asshole at this moment."

I nodded that he was right.

"Out of your mind," offered Schroeder. "I'm warning you as a friend."

"Yes? Maybe . . . yes, out of my mind. Agreed. Asshole, yes! And did I tell you that on the last day of the festival, at the last supper in that crappy schnitzel place you took us all to, she whispered in my ear that when I do my book tour stop in Berlin I should plan to dine in her home?"

"But that didn't mean she loves you. She invites a lot of writers to her house. She's ambitious. She probably fucks half of them. Hans told me she never has women writers over, just men. She's a cock cannibal. And by the time of this invitation you already knew that she was married, of course. So, what gave you the idea that if you dined with this vicious tart, it would all work out? It must have been clear to you by the third day of the festival that she is no good."

"The text she sent. She sent two. In the first she wrote, "Remember: come for dinner." But the next night, she sent a second text which read, "The day after dinner you and I will pick chestnuts in the little park behind my house." I looked at him meaningfully. "Chestnuts, okay? What does THAT tell you?"

"Chestnuts? What the fuck?! That told you something? Chestnuts??? What does it tell me? It tells me that you have a chestnut for a brain. How does chestnuts translate into 'I want to desert my marriage, drop my lover, and spend the rest of my life with you?' What are you, a squirrel? Maybe it just means that she planned to pick chestnuts and bake them in a pie."

I looked him hard in the eyes. "Trust me on this, Schroeder: that's not what chestnuts meant."

But Schroeder, who must have been a real sonofabitch as an insurance man, his face a moat against the grief of widows and hunger tears of orphans, wasn't having any of it.

Shifting to "Not My Department" mode, Schroeder quickly changed the subject to Edwin, whom I was about to meet, his oldest friend and like himself a former insurance executive but smarter for having left government service to launch and build his own private firm into a huge success which he then sold off for several million euros. I could easily understand poor Schroeder's envy-tinged admiration, for after retirement he himself became a literary publisher—by definition, in today's world, a 'loser.'

Apparently, at the sale of Edwin's firm a dozen or so loyal employees got dumped by the new owners into the street. Edwin, already on a yacht sailing for Cabo, left behind completely penniless out-of-work families. Not His Problem. He now lived in retirement, drinking himself into incontinence and lavishing vast sums on prostitution, which is legal in Austria, though subject to codified restrictions cleverly tailored to the character and economies of the various cities, towns, and regions where the night ladies stroll. Salzburg is famed for its brothels, some of which date back to the time of Mozart, who, though married, spent huge gobs of his small fortune on whores and died broke.

I absorbed all this in silence, nodded with an appreciative smile, to show respect for this Edwin's motley history. "A man after my own heart," I said half-jokingly.

"He will cure you of this disease of Lena. You will see."

Chapter 10

As we lapsed into observation of the boulevards before us, the constant parade of high-heeled women clicking past our voracious inspection, Edwin showed up, a man of great molecular density, with leathery suntanned skin and a debauched bacchanalian face. He reeked of evil. His huge hands were feral animals. Dressed in a collarless white pilot's shirt, blue jeans, and sandals, he came up slyly at first, pretending shyness, but in his eyes was the unconcealable look of a mad dog. For this reason, I liked Edwin instantly.

Those who breaststroke in the abyss always interest me. His smile made clear: there is nothing he won't do. Regardless of how depraved, if that's what his genitals wanted, consider it done. Clearly those nuts, not his brain, were in charge. I would not have been surprised had he turned out to be a serial killer and, because I have a soft side for villains, would have wanted to know him even more for it. He was a full-fledged pervert, that much was clear, with the hale constitution and twisted penchants of the generations of inbred sheep-raping Jew-hating Tyrolean mountaineers from which he descended.

Schroeder said to Edwin, "This is my famous Nathan Falk. You should be honored, you filthy mutt, to meet such a literary eminence.

Edwin studied me appraisingly. "Is it true that you once served in the Israeli army?"

I nodded.

His face showed mingled distaste and respect. "But why? You are an American, no?"

"Since your people killed my people, I grew up wanting to be a Jewish soldier. So, I went, I served; your kind will never kill my kind again. End of story."

He chuckled. "But weren't you afraid? You could have been killed."

I shrugged. "It would have been a good death."

"Isn't Falk wonderful?" said Schroeder, but Edwin ignored him, stared at me, then said, "That is something I would never do. Not for anyone. To die for some country. You gotta be kidding."

"But for a whore you would destroy yourself," said Schroeder, winking at me.

At the mention of whores, a crazed look lit Edwin's face. "The most beautiful whores in Austria are from East and Central Europe: Russians, Ukrainians, Poles, Hungarians, Czechs, Serbs, Croats, Latvians, and so on. Women with creamy skin and alabaster bodies like Rodin sculptures. Women with modest, submissive manners and tricky eyes who are there to drive you out of your mind with pleasure in order to get their pretty red nails on your credit card. But the cost has broken me, sent me to the poorhouse. I haven't got a cent left."

Schroeder made a face. "Don't exaggerate! You've got more than a cent or two." And turning to me, he said, "I told you, he sold his company for millions."

"And spent every cent on whores. They've taken everything."

"It's true," said Schroeder. "He spends what he has on them."

"Not just one," Edwin said. "Two, three, four at a time. A bed full of whores is a wonderful thing, my friend. You, Falk, your name sounds like *fuck*. You should give this to yourself at least once. Imagine being an infant with many hungry adoring young mothers pleasuring every inch of your baby flesh. Imagine three of them taking turns on you with their mouths. It feels like God."

"So, God is a bed full of whores." I smiled and winked at Schroeder. "I think you've solved mankind's most agonized philosophical conundrum: What is God? Where is He? And all along, he was in the brothels of Salzburg. Who knew?"

"I don't believe in that religious shit," said Schroeder. "Do you, Falk? It's not the first time I've heard you mention His name. I'm beginning to worry."

"I think—this is just my opinion—that human beings are

living proof of the existence of God, yet ironically, we think that we are proof that He does not exist. Well, whether or not He exists, the fact remains that we do have an inbuilt need for some kind of deity. That need is expressed everywhere, in every culture, every part of the world, and no more so than among the disbelievers who devote their whole lives to proving the nonexistence of God."

"That sounds very pretty, Mr. Fuck, the Great Writer," said Edwin disdainfully. "But I don't know what the hell you're talking about. And if whores were God, I would bang them twice as hard. But those whores are not God. They are greedy rats with tight cunts who have taken everything from me. I can't afford them anymore. So, I've stopped going. And I'm lonely for them." He looked stricken.

Schroeder glanced at me, winked, and then turned his bemused gaze back at Edwin. "How long since you've stopped."

"Since this morning," Edwin said in complete seriousness. Schroeder and I burst out laughing.

"Falk. If as you say we humans were created to underscore the existential mystery of God, then Edwin, who is the Pope of Prostitutes, was created to prove the eternal need for whores."

"Tell me, Edwin, how much for the less expensive tricks?" I asked.

"Seventy euros for thirty minutes. A half and half. Or, blow job and quick fuck. But why waste money? It's worth it to pay a little more for the best. Go a full hour with a Russian or Pole. Then, you're living! If they like you, they fuck with juice. They'll appreciate you. You're a pretty one. They'll eat you up and let you go down on them. Their pussies taste like pudding. What do you like?"

"Skinny blondes," I said.

He nodded gravely, a real pro. "I'll see what I can do."

"He's serious," said Schroeder. "He knows every whore in Salzburg. Also, Innsbruck, Graz, and Vienna."

"And I've slept with every one of them more than once," said Edwin proudly. He leaned over to Schroeder and whispered.

Schroeder looked up. "He invites us to lunch. He has already made the reservation."

"Good. I could use a big schnitzel," I said.

"Schnitzel," Schroeder laughed, shaking his head. "My great author can use a big Schnitzel."

We walked along several broad tree-lined boulevards, three worthless and imbecilic men with nothing better to do, who knew how little we counted for in the scheme of things and didn't care. We stopped in a hole-in-the wall tavern so small at most it couldn't have held more than ten customers. In there, hunched over drinks and so close to conversation that their shoulders touched, were four regulars, and by the look of their cauliflower noses, blurred eyeballs, and haggard faces, all clearly were hard-drinking retirees of some sort, their mates dead or divorced, their useful employments kaput, and ever-so-slowly and comfortably rowing to an early grave thanks to well-stocked pensions and secure investments. They greeted Edwin with veteran nods of bitter disaffection and did not budge from their stations. The barkeeper, a buxom blonde with a deadpan face but saucy eyes, gazed appraisingly at me and smiled. Put a few drinks in her and she'd be wonderful trouble to have on one's hands.

Edwin stopped to talk to a slender sharp-edged man in his seventies with cold white hair framing a red unpleasant face who addressed him with a bitter look of amusement. Edwin replied heatedly. I thought a fight would erupt. A whispery hissing short-tempered exchange flared, inaudible to any but the combatants. An old broad who had once been beautiful—I could tell—in an aristocratic sort of way (but now looked frayed, unkept, lost in drunken neglect) aimed theatrical barbed looks at their close-bent bickering faces, and then looked up at us with mock vaudevillian disgust. This spat ignited yet more laughter and Schroeder leaned close to my ear, said, "The old shit with white hair is the former chief of police for all of Salzburg. Edwin and he are drinking pals. And the woman, she used to be an important politician in this town. Now look at her!" Schroeder chuckled with a look of amazed disdain.

"Look at the two great friends," she called out loudly to the chief of police and Edwin, "one the most corrupt cop in Salzburg's history and the other the worst pimp in all of Austria. How touching!"

More snorting laughter from the others.

"Is it true?" I asked Schroeder "Edwin is a pimp?"

Schroeder shrugged with a wicked smile. "Who knows? I wonder sometimes."

On the scuffed brown cupboard behind the bar hung a calendar pinup of a naked woman positioned to receive a lover frontally and it was really quite lewd and yet erotically shot, and the barkeep, noticing my fascination, said, "You would like one like this?" and nodded toward Edwin. "You're with the right person, if one can even call him a person." Then, suddenly, the former prominent politician broke in, "But he deals only in the cheapest bitches," to which Edwin shot back, "I tried to trick you on the streets, didn't I? But no takers! Not even from the Montenegrins, who fuck goats! You can't blame me if even the goat-fuckers don't want your sunless white ass!" and again, harsh laughter and Schroeder leaning close, "They all love Edwin in here."

After shaking hands all around we walked out and along a grand boulevard with eighteenth-century white hat-box buildings and rich tourists in hot pants, high heels, and sunglasses, or Orvis tee shirts, sun hats, and cargo shorts. I thought of Lena at home with Hubert, her husband, doing laundry, or Skyping with Rolf, putting the finishing touches on her book, despairing of the future, and making trouble on social media with politically incorrect, outrageous posts about everything from Putin to Trump to Andy Warhol to the need for men to change from standing to seated when peeing. The surest way to reach her, see her, was on Skype, the free online feed for face to face chats and to which she is so addicted that she carries her tablet around with her everywhere in order to be instantly available.

I had first Skyped her from a hotel in Zurich, an unbearable experience. She had installed Skype on my laptop during the three days I spent in her Berlin home. I remember that when I reached her for the very first time by this method there she was, magically, and so deliciously beautiful, with finger to lips, a warning not to speak, and typing an SMS message that appeared in a blue balloon beside her face: "Hubert is home. We must be silent." And then she smiled mischievously, whirled her face around, sent hair flying into a wild halo, and opened her blouse to show her breasts on which she laid hands over her heart to signal her love. I SMSed back, "I'm dying of love for you but, still, you're going away with Rolf, aren't you?" She hesitated, grim now, and nodded sadly so that tears shot from my eyes and involuntarily I blurted out, "Sorry, but I can't seem to help myself." Her finger shot to her lips so quickly I tapped into the keys, "I have to get off," and she wrote back, "Okay," and after she had spun away into offscreen darkness she sent me the emoji of a hugging teddy bear. Interesting, I thought, that she still hasn't ever actually said that she loves me— so what did this kitschy Japanese anime icon signify? Did it mean, 'Take comfort, child. Yes, I will betray you but a part of me is like a mother to you now and you should accept my love, however it's given . . . ?'" But then what, I wondered, as I walked: be loved, yes, but also betrayed? What animated emoji would she then send for my breaking heart? On Skype they have a round yellow weeping face that somehow, for me, does not quite convey the depth of my suffering by Lena. What image, I wondered as I walked, can convey the unendurable emotional torture that I feel every minute, when either apart from her or in her presence? Did she really expect me to wait for her while she traipsed around the tropics with her lover? Did she really expect me, on her return, to join her?

Chapter 11

In the restaurant, on the outdoor patio, a lone attractive brunette with bright red lipstick and dressed in a tight red tank top, white pants, and red high-heeled slippers rose to greet us. Smiling with unconcealed sarcasm, Edwin said to me, "Trude, my wife." Trude charmingly took my hand, held it for an instant, passing warmth to me, and said, "I read the translation of your book. It's wonderful. Welcome." Then she and Schroeder, old friends, pecked cheeks and we all sat down.

Menus were opened but I barely looked at mine. Instead I studied Edwin, one of those creatures who make an immediate first impression. Gradually, his character revealed itself, and sensing the malevolence in him, my amusement turned to alarm. He is, for instance, far more thickset than I had first realized, and even more densely muscular; his face, highlighted by a trim pointy vandyke, is heavy, massive even, and again, saturnine, debauched, quite cruel, Bacchus gone to the devil. Face to face, Edwin's sinister expression entices you to a knife fight, the alley-gleam of a barber's razor.

After lunch, we strolled some more, pointlessly, aimlessly, which seemed to be the principle occupation of many people in Salzburg, mostly the idle rich, and I didn't know where we were headed, no one seemed to have an interest in telling me, and I didn't ask as it didn't seem to matter. Nothing in Salzburg seemed to matter. Nothing whatever.

Every so often I glanced at Edwin who did not walk alongside his wife though she kept glancing anxiously at him.

Schroeder and I walked along together. "Look at how she follows behind him, like an Arab woman," grinned Schroeder.

"I can't believe he's married to a doll like that and cheats on her with tramps."

"You are naïve," said Schroeder. "Most married men in Austria want tramps."

"But why Edwin?"

"Especially Edwin."

"He's powerfully built."

"He is from the mountain peasants. They are indestructible. And stubborn. And crazy. And they believe crazy things. They think that Jews have secret stores of hidden gold somewhere in the Alps. Now and then a stupid mountaineer is killed searching for it."

"I don't like how he treats Trude. No one should treat his lover like that."

"He treats all women that way. When he drinks, you must be careful. He gets violent. Sometimes he hits the whores."

"Don't the pimps jump in?"

Schroeder seemed to weigh his answer carefully. "When Edwin is in the room there is only one pimp: Edwin."

"So, he IS a pimp!"

Schroeder shrugged evasively. "I'm just speaking colorfully. You know, he could have been an SS guard in a concentration camp. He's just lucky to have been born after '45. He is that type. Brutal. A bit of a sadist. The kind who laughs as he hurts you."

But the still greater shock came when we turned, suddenly, into a nondescript building and ascended to the most spectacular apartment I have ever visited, its walls lined with original Pop Art, a few millions worth—Lichtenstein, Warhol, Jasper Johns, Rauschenberg, original sculpture from Oldenburg, and all the furnishing done in sixties mod decor. One entire wall opened onto a balcony facing a cliff atop which stood a palace and, beneath, the roofs of Salzburg, while directly across the way, glimpsed through a scrim of trees, an immense ancient tower clock kept time, rotating on the hour life-sized figurines of dairy maids in aprons who performed pretty little mechanical pirou- ettes as gongs chimed an alpine tune. We stretched out on deep white leather chairs, looked out on all of this, and sipped from cups of aromatic cinnamon-flavored coffee, prepared and served by Trude. I leaned over to Schroeder, whispered, "How does he afford this? Running whores?"

Schroeder looked up at me meaningfully.

Chapter 12

I had succeeded so far to avoid contacting Lena, stayed completely offline, needing a break from her, possibly permanent. Gerhardt, who had set up the event for me, met me at the Literaturhaus early and we embraced like the old dear friends that we are. A crowd had started to gather.

Several times he'd visited me in San Francisco, where I keep a barely used pied-à-terre, preferring to stay on the move, give readings, write in hotels, accept grants, meet women, have brief affairs in which no one gets too badly hurt, though after they end sometimes I lay for days curled up fetus-like in bed. Gerhardt lives as I do, dedicated to writing at the expense of all else and consequently we are a pair of miserable bastards, which we openly acknowledge to each other.

As a European writer, though, he earns far more money, has the greater reputation, and is treated with a deference that would stun American writers. Still, as writers who hold each other in high regard, we don't care about such things very much. It's the writing that matters. Otherwise, we couldn't be friends. Consequently, we have few other writer friends.

Of course, he knows all about Lena. In several long and rambling emails, I had kept him apprised. Always, he responded calmly and gently, trying to inject some common sense into me, which failed. He has short-cropped hair, searching gray-blue eyes, a strong jaw supporting a carefully cultivated perpetual five o' clock shadow, and his usual garb, indifferent to style, is a rumpled sports jacket, polo shirt, chinos, and shabby tennis shoes. To see him you would not think that he has won every single major award given for German and Austrian literature. He looks, instead, like a ski bum.

Leaning close, he said, "And Lena?"

The question moistened my eyes, which he saw. He nodded. "Say no more. Let me go over there to kiss my editor. I'm happy she came. I'll be right back."

I nodded. A good thirty minutes remained before the program's start, more than enough time to compose myself. But for now, I had no wish to do so; instead I wanted to go somewhere private, weep inside, silently, invisibly. I asked the Literaturhaus's director, Joachim, if there was someplace that I could be alone for a bit, reflect, and ground myself, before things started.

"Of course!" he said and led me to his office, to his large oak desk. "Please, sit here. Be comfortable. May I say, Nathan, how very glad we feel to have you back with us? Your last appearance was so well received."

"I'm glad to be here. Thank you, Joachim."

"I will leave you to your thoughts." He glanced at his watch, the sleeve of his black suit jacket riding up his snow-white wrist. "In about twenty-five minutes can you please take the stage? Do you wish for a reminder?"

"No. That's fine. See you onstage."

"Very good," he smiled sadly, for I think he must have caught something profoundly forlorn in my face, if only for just an instant.

Chapter 13

A nd so I sit, not visibly shedding tears but weeping inside, recalling Lena, in her little car, parked outside a museum in the stone-brown sooty rain of a Berlin night. The museum's walls appeared stained with tears as from a dirty graveyard angel. Lena's innocent face was framed by blue-white blotches of random pulsing light that shadowed and circled her silky long chestnut brown hair as she turned to me in the front seat with soft small hand in mine, her inclining head surrendered to my shoulder. If only she would rest there, if only my hand could softly slip along the sweet curve of Lena's cheek which she, in turn, would press tenderly, firmly, against my palm, nuzzling like a little dove and sending a current of electrifying tenderness between her skin and mine, our flesh fused as one, born to be together, same cells—even our hands identical, just on a different scale.

And if, in that car, I wept, it was because I had to leave her, if only temporarily, though for how long was at that point impossible to say, and because it was a good-bye, I wished that everyone and anyone intimately connected to her life—Hubert, her husband, her front-rank lover Rolf, other occasional paramours named Bodo, Wolfe, Sigmund, Theodoric (and one, incredibly, named Hansel, about whom, each one, she spoke in detail, including the occasional graphic descriptions of the size and shape of each one's particular member)—should understand that their being with her was all one big mistake, that from birth, even before then, she and I have belonged to each other; but that by dint of random circumstance, the confluence of war, history, poverty, anti-Semitism, disease, social disorder, she and I were unjustly kept apart, unknown to each other, separated by tens of thousands of miles—but now, all has changed: by divine right she is mine. Now, everyone, all her suitors, past, present and future, should go home, leave us be.

But none of them knew of me in her life. I chose insanely to believe that she and I understood what we meant for each other, though it's possible that even she didn't know what was in my head—that only I and I alone bore the secret burden of our love. In the director's office, as in her car in Berlin, a savage wave of unanswerable loss rose to my eyes, watered my sorrow, convulsed my chest. I wept unabashedly, as I had done, repeatedly, since setting eyes on her.

Why must love and loss so intimately intertwine? How can it be that one whom I was born to love and be loved by now plans to jet off to Latin America with some jerk whom she claims no longer to love or even particularly to desire, and to spend three months with him touring, copulating, while I sit in hotel rooms waiting, destroyed a little more each day? How can it be?

"Don't be so emotional," she had once said on Skype. "You're like a teenaged child. Don't make so much drama out of this. Write me a poem. Be joyful. You're making me feel like a piece of shit."

On her bed, in her studio, in the afternoons, when Hubert was gone, we would lie eye to eye embracing, gazing into each other, silent—just breathing together was enough—and then we would rise and adjourned to the kitchen to nurse cups of hot tea, hold hands, and smile. When I weep silently inside it is to recall how it felt to kiss strands of her hair perched on my fingertips, to whisper close to her baby-soft ear, hold her wrapped in my arms, like wings of a fierce protective hawk or angel.

Fastening a few shirt buttons, tightening my belt, I walked out of the office, passed down a corridor, turned left, found the director and Gerhardt waiting in the wings. Out there was a massive audience, a full house. The director met my approach with a look of exasperated relief.

"Are we all set?" he asked no one in particular, staring straight ahead.

"Yes."

"Lead on," said Gerhardt.

Ushered onto the stage before a large crowd, we took our seats with amused gravity, clearly aware of our self-evident authority (though nicely understated in our relaxed body language as we adjusted our microphones and waited out the director's introduction), whereupon Gerhardt turned to me with the first question: "Why do you write?"

Me: "Because life is a heartbreaking deception."

Gerhardt: "And what might that deception be?"

Me: "Deceived by the idea that love as we would feel it, love that truly would gratify us in the very pit of our being, is at all possible. Well, it is not. It doesn't exist."

Gerhardt: "Not at all?"

Me: "No. Not at all."

Gerhardt: "And yet, love is the principle conversation topic in the world. More is written about love than any other subject, even war. Why would the world expend so much energy on something that doesn't exist?"

Me: "Because we hope that it exists, even though no one in the history of the world has ever felt loved in response to their need for it. Everyone, from the beginning of time, has felt, in the pit of their being, disappointed. But it is unbearable to think that, so it is denied; from the beginning of time, everyone has felt disappointed, let down, alienated even, but afraid to admit it. It is the very reason why there is and will always be war after war. Men make war when the absence of love reaches fever pitch. Then come the guns and the rise of empires. We may need love just to survive, but it is intangible, like God, beyond reach, a thing we crave, hunt after, strive for, and hope for, because we have been cruelly instilled with this terrible need for it but in the end, it's no use. We cannot have it. We will never have it. To the very last day of our lives that sense which has always stalked and tormented us—the feeling that we have never really known more than the most fleeting connection to another human being—remains, cruelly unhealed, unbearable, so terrible that it is inadmissible, the great truth of this life: love does not exist. We live as though love exists. We pretend. John Lennon writes a song; we hum it to ourselves, in our hearts: 'Love is real, real is love.' Then Mark David

Chapman's bullets rip through Lennon's flesh. That's pretty real. Still, defiant, we talk about love. Make films about it, write books. But in our hearts, we know we are alone, unloved, and we no more know as adults where love is to be had than we do where God is to be found."

Gerhardt looked at me, surprised: "That's a very interesting but also a quite devastating perspective."

Me: "I don't think so. It's simply true. The later existentialist writers—I mean after Dostoyevsky, Kierkegaard—like Sartre, Beckett, Kafka, Camus, and so forth, very clearly saw that. Their mistake was to interpret the nonexistence of love as the nonexistence of God. But what if God exists but not love? God=love is Christianity. Certainly, the stories in the Torah make no such claim. Of course, one can act 'as if' love exists; make it up as you go along. That, for the most part, is what 'good people' do. But the religious codification of love is bullshit. Ironically, love, in the modern era, is firmly believed to be essential to our existence. I claim that it is not. Why? Because despite all the beaming white-hairs spewing love from the pews of the worship houses, in this world there is no love. No one has ever given love to another in a way that feels authentic, feels real. There have been deeds, yes, tokens, sure, and a trillion declarations, but has anyone else actually felt loved for all those superficial gestures? No. At most, some have felt euphoric rushes of pheremone-driven delusions of love or self-absorbed outbursts of temporary gratitude for rescue but that is no more than a chemical rush to the brain. Then the catalytic effect wears off, the hormonal drug high lessens, then dissipates. Today's love-drunk paramour is tomorrow's haunted and embittered solitary individual huddled under awnings in the rain. The initial feeling is not love; it is an ejaculation. And what follows should the fool hang on is only the stubborn postponement of the inevitable letdown. And it does come. The crash and burn are horrific."

And so forth and so on.

And as I sat pouring out this hideous stuff, I felt a horrifying surge of bilious grief course through me, right into my tear ducts from which mortifying rivulets of shame sprang down my cheeks but I kept talking, and Gerhardt, taken aback, stopped, gaped, reached into his jacket pocket, produced a handkerchief, handed it to me. "Are you all right?" he inquired gently, every eye in the audience riveted to my wet face (no one in history has ever held an audience more captive to his agonized pronouncements).

"Yes, I'm fine," I declared loudly, blowing my nose.

"Are you sure?"

"Sure? Why, NO! I'm NOT fucking sure!" I howled. And I turned on the audience, gripping the arms of my chair like an orangutan set to spring among them with razor clenched in teeth and slash madly every which way, shrieking out the name of Edgar Allen Poe. "Do you really think I write because I want to? As some kind of wish fulfillment? Writing is not my fucking TRADE! My books are the footprints of extreme emergencies. I write about what it feels like to be a child who is alternately loved and beaten by his mother because her experiences in the Holocaust drove her mad, as well they should have! I write about what it feels like at the age of eight to discover that before my birth, people—Austrians and the Germans in particular—slaughtered six million of my kin—men, women, children—and that really no one has ever paid for the crime. Furthermore, the descendants of the killers—whole nations of killers, really—Germany, Austria, Poland, Hungary, France, Lithuania, Italy, Ukraine, and many more—even the people in this room—not only live as though it never occurred but sit here talking about love and go out to vilify the Jews of Israel with smug so-called 'Progressive' postmodern notions of political truth unaffirmed by any sense of reality. Some of them even justify killing Jews all over again! In Sweden, they chant 'Kill the Jews!' In England! France! Norway! Denmark! Italy! Gray-haired ponytailed European Union Progressives standing shoulder to shoulder in front of Israeli consulates with anti-Semitic genocidal Hamasniks and pro-regime Iranians, pumping their fists under banners that display the swastika superimposed on the Star of David screaming, "Save

Gaza, Kill Jews!" and "One Bullet, One Jew!" and "Gaza=Warsaw Ghetto!"

"Can you imagine? Yes, no doubt, because some of you here probably have joined those demonstrations. I mean what the fuck is that? That is love? You murder six million of my kind and now we are going to talk about love? We are going to have love? We are going to be healed? We are going to write touching stories, produce heartfelt films, and copulate in the bedroom and buy wedding rings and declare our union sacrosanct before the world, even though, statistically, within two years we'll either be fucking a coworker on a business trip or taking or giving it from behind in a bar bathroom? When somewhere in the cold hard earth of Europe the bone of the slaughtered Jew yet disintegrates? You can find Jew bone chips in the ponds and fields around Auschwitz and the other death camps. You, all of you, have turned time into obscenity. History itself has become your 'Get Out of Jail' card. You have made of normal life a disgrace, for in an age of mass graves conformity and anonymity are crimes. Everyone must have their fifteen minutes. Everyone's existence is a selfie. Facebook is the result of Treblinka, Babi Yar, Chelimo, where the very notion of human individuation perished in gas chambers and mass graves! What does it say about us that after such a monumental horror normal life can proceed on or offline, as though nothing had occurred? To live normally after Treblinka is itself a crime! There should be no normal life. We should stop living normally at once. You with your terrible drive for normalcy! Your normalcy is a crime!"

Gerhardt smiled stiffly. "And do what instead?" For in his way, he too, with his model, if Mailer-like, literary career, was an agent of normalcy.

"To begin with, rend your garments, tear out your hair, claw your cheeks with fingernails until they bleed, and weep and scream and shout in your Reichstag, which you must rename! Start over. You love dogs so much, cute little ones especially. Make them your leaders. Put yourselves on leashes. Let them walk you! Enslave you to their whims, though whenever I see you stoop with an inverted plastic grocery bag scooping up their shit from side-walks, I recognize that to some degree they already rule you. But imagine if dogs led us. For any one of them would make a better leader then our current crop. What would life be then? Play! Running around under open skies, chasing tossed balls and frisbees. Munching on healthy foods and treats. Getting our bellies rubbed, cooing out tender nonsense. We'd all have cute nicknames!! For dogs know what love is. Dogs know HOW to love! We must tear down this evil world, tear it down and model ourselves after dogs. Normal life should be something that humanity as a whole must learn from dogs rather than the corrupt model conferred upon baby humans, poisoning them from birth on. All 'normal life' must instantly cease! This is my preference: that all Gentiles enter upon a cycle of global mourning, a Middle Age of perpetual penitence punctuated by fasting and mortifications of the flesh. When enough time has been passed in this fashion, we will declare the healed Gentile a dog and permit him to enter upon the dog's life of licking hands, pissing and shitting in public, and eating out of bowls. We will give them an actual dog to rule over them."

"Who is this 'We' you refer to?"

"We Jews," I smiled.

Gerhardt looked dumbstruck. The audience stirred uncom-fortably.

"You cannot, after the Holocaust, allow life to go on as it does, relentlessly, remorselessly, pitilessly, as though nothing happened. Some talk of the German nation's—the world's—efforts at peni-tence! Don't make me laugh! Instead, in an unrepentant Europe, we have Internet porn, naked Aryan models plastered across buses and billboards, nude sunbathing, and at soccer matches glittery women parade around in high heels posing their *bundesflagge*-painted and shaved pudenda. I see mass graves in the anonymous condos springing up everywhere. Lunatic Mussolini prototypes are winning office everywhere. The world is preoccupied with pregnant film stars, but flips past news about the little Jewish girl whose brains are blown out by a jihadist in the courtyard of a French Jewish day school, the Christian child crucified by the

Islamic State, the Jordanian pilot videotaped ablaze in an iron cage. Instead, your surfing mouse is in a big rush to click on the online shoe store sale. So, I write about the barely noted atrocities, the uncared-for murdered. I write about how the world does not give a fuck, does not even deserve to be called the world or humanity or even dogmanity. I write about me, about a child's needs unmet by a Holocaust survivor mother who can barely keep herself from jumping out the window and about how it feels to be an alienated Israeli soldier who must battle a sea of people intent upon his annihilation and about those others who with furious indignation protest against him and accuse and judge him. And I write about what it's like to be a horrible drunk who crawls out of a bottle one day, detoxing and hallucinating, in order to survive."

"Are you a horrible drunk?"

"Put a drink in me and you'll see. But I've been clean and sober now for years."

Applause. Always, there is that: their chance to show a little love for the rehabilitated profligate, the hopeful American game show contestant competing for their ecstatically appreciative audience applause and the grand prize of their evaporating sympathy.

And yet, for that other matter—the one about gas chambers and smashing Jewish skulls with crowbars and hammers in public squares and feeding entire Jewish families, oftentimes alive, to the insatiable flames of the crematoria—for that mostly they just sit, these German-speaking audiences, in poker-faced remorseless silence unless there are a few Jews among them who nod my way with furtive smiles, thrilled to hear such things said but not wishing to stand out, by their appreciation, alone in the crowd. No one wants to be alone in a crowd.

"And what is the emergency you're presently writing about?"

My lips part to speak but close on silence. And within me as though some secret dumb waiter door has slid shut, all the subterranean lights click off, and there I am, a pure essential *being*, witness to *nothingness*, and not a single mousey feeling nor dusty tumble of thought stirs in the midnight of my veins, nor does a single atomized spectral wisp of airborne incarnated human expression materialize as from a poltergeist anywhere in my vicinity but rather just nothing reposes behind my eyeballs, my irises sunk like submerged dead divers and there's absolutely no more for the audience to hear from me.

Yet, they wait. And Gerhardt waits. Then, one of his sneakered feet slides softly off the stage floor, and lifting a finger to his cheek, he taps it nervously, smiles, turns to the audience, and says, "A writer reflects," which invites chuckles; then he turns back to me—I, who sit there open-mouthed, dumbstruck, agape—and says, "You seem deep in thought. Are you? If so, about what?"

Red-eyed, my tired face the wasted aftermath of sorrow, I say, "Love. Despite that love is impossible, yet, still, I love. And how she, the beloved, responds feels not like love. It feels like death. In that way, at least, she is honest. She knows that love cannot be experienced by the other party involved and so doesn't bother to try. She turns her giving of love, the only form of love available to transact with, as a form of punishment, a torment, an affliction, an act of revenge. She repays overtures of love with suffering and pain."

The transfixed audience stares.

More questions asked. More answers to the unanswerable. The conversation turns to other writers whom I mentally consult in the course of composing my "prose emergencies": Hubert Selby Jr., whom I knew; I. B. Singer, whom I met; Knut Hamsun; Jack Kerouac, whose daughter, Jan, I knew; Joseph Conrad; Charles Bukowski, whom I published with; Fyodor Dostoyevsky.

"And yet," I say, "I am nothing at all like them. That is part of my trouble. I am always only myself, no other, inescapably so, and have no example to consult or emulate. I am that which I seek liberation from, the Me who needs You, even as I am not yet what I most want to become: the one whose prose can someday destroy all of you. For none of you deserve to live, nor does this world deserve existence. But because I, too, live among you in this world and continue, absurdly, to long for love, still believing that some marriage of two beings who quite naturally belong to each other is yet possible, to exist in perpetual consanguineous dialogue of language and flesh, flying around in each other's arms like a couple of Chagall figures, swooning, happy . . ."

My face drops. My hand lifts, palm out, like a traffic cop, to stop their eyes from looking, seeing the tears. And I turn my back to them, sit perfectly still, shoulders hunched, head lowered. Charlie Parker paused, playing silence to the crowd.

Gerhardt faces the audience, eyebrows lifted in wonder. "Ladies and gentlemen, Nathan Falk!"

They explode in applause, cheers, come to their feet for the shocking three-ring Jew of ineffectual Holocaustic fury. A two-hour historical lecture appealing to their rational understanding would have failed just as miserably. There is no reaching them. The Literaturhaus's event planning team has scored a win. Satisfied, entertained, the crowd files into the rotunda to line up at a book table stacked high with copies of my books. This part of each event is a nightmare. I must sit there like a sex robot version of my authorial persona, smiling seductively, autographing their purchases, cooing nice words, again and again, one after the other, a hostess to the Johns, my brain screeching with rage, as exhausted as a whore's cunt. It's dehumanizing. Denigrating. Positively sickening. My soul cries out against it.

The money, though, is good.

Chapter 14

After, we converge. Gerhardt, the director, myself, as well as several staff members and Schroeder, cluster together and pass through the main rotunda like a self-important entourage of Inquisition officials en route to the torture chamber, drunk on our own lusty and murderous gravitas, arbiters of literary taste and direction, and enter through a tall door into a narrow corridor lined with offices in one of which takes place the absurdly cere-monious signing of tax documents, and the handing over to myself and Gerhardt envelopes bulging with cash. Our author fees. We then all go out to dinner, courtesy of the Literaturhaus.

Until now, no one speaks of the farce that has transpired on stage. Why should they? It's done. The audience leaves scandalized and satisfied. They'll have something to gnaw on for weeks. Stacks of books sold. Who cares if the guest author dropped his trouser and took a dump in their faces? So long as the ticket buyers feel they got their euro's worth, *alles gut!*

But en route to dine, as we stroll through the streets, Gerhardt sidles over and, leaning his face next to my ear, snickers, "That was truly outrageous."

Wanly, I nod, grin. "Was it?"

"No, really. It was fantastic. I have never . . . they will speak of this in Salzburg for days to come."

Again, a weak rueful smile. "Do you really think so?"

"Tomorrow, we will see in *Der Standard* some sort of write-up. I'm sure there will be outrage."

"How do you know?"

"Their reporter was in the audience. His pen moved like crazy. You will see."

"Great," I said without enthusiasm.

"You are all right then? I know you felt deeply but a small part of this must have been a bit of a performance, no? I mean, you didn't do anything like this in your other appearances, yes? I imagine you made a decision to change approach. Well, it worked!"

"I made no such decision. The only change is that I'm more fucked up now than ever over Lena. I think I'm having a nervous breakdown. And it's spilling over into my professional life."

"Then it's even more amazing," said Gerhardt. "It just comes out of you so naturally. Such sincerity. And depth. It's marvelous."

Lena and I adore each other but at some point she and Rolf will undress and embrace. She will fellate him. He will then mount her and penetrate. She will slide her vagina back and forth over his blood-engorged urinary implement. They will kiss and kiss and stroke and pant and moan and pound and arch and quiver and clench and erupt in spasmodic ejaculations. They will softly kiss over and over and over and over as fervor fades, to be replaced by the velvet whispering viscidity of love's afterglow and they will smile and they will touch and they will talk and peck, nibble and tongue, and jump from bed to go eat something, and return with it contained in Styrofoam, and sit naked, cross-legged, genitals agape, leaning into each other, inserting food between each other's lips, and then stretch out embracing and lie happily together. No matter what pretty lies she tells me I know that it will be so on their little three-month jaunt through South American jungles.

That is why, in part, I am turning internally into a primaeval tropical hell—a dark, dank, swampish, muddy inferno traversed by shrieking parrots ablaze with garish color, obscene spider monkeys with bared teeth, Mandrills snarling with furious red gums, their murderous black nostrils inflamed. My soul steals through dense impassable undergrowth, crawling over atrocious insects waddling and creeping about in their armor-plated gelatinous toxicity. I am intent upon no less than murder. An urge to kill Lena hides deep within the swampish everglade in which I squat weeping, caked with mud, my apish organ erect—and on the ground some dead beast that I have slain purely from outrage and have no intention of eating. My fat black leathery finger digs deep within a hideous trembling wound still alive with senseless ticking like the immense clock overlooking Edwin's flat as senseless satyrs laugh and roar evilly through the Salzburgian jungle night.

And after dining out Gerhardt and I return to the Literaturhaus, repair upstairs for lattes, and there in the lounge, waiting, find none other than Edwin, his lovely wife, and a slender, terrifically-stacked blonde with a come-fuck-me-face but who seems to be just a touch too sweet to be a whore. I am wrong. She is a whore whom Edwin has recruited to bed me.

"So," Edwin says to me, slightly drunk and swaying as the staffers look on in astonishment. "This is what you like, yes? Skinny blonde, high heels. Greta, stand up! Show the famous author what you've got."

"Don't be ridiculous," sniffs Greta. She offers me her hand decorously, like one to the manor born, which Edwin finds enticingly provocative, for suddenly it is all too clear that Edwin has no intention of sharing his little blondie with anyone, wants her all to himself, has used the prospect of screwing a "famous" author to lure her here.

Revolted, fascinated, the director and staff retreat from the room. Gerhardt, intrigued, lingers, but then quite sensibly quits the scene. He returned, I later learned, to his hotel.

Hard to say just why I felt responsible for the girl, for the whole preposterous situation. If anyone, Schroeder, who had told Edwin about the reading, should have asked these misfits to leave at once. But that wasn't Schroeder's way. Big, jolly, sly, Schroeder maintained a neat remove from the unfolding catastrophe—it was Not His Department—yet he derived the maximum voyeuristic perv amusement from what was going on.

"I told you," he said, leaning close to my ear. "Put a few drinks into Edwin and this is what you get. He's actually insane."

Certainly, Edwin now seemed so, looming over the young whore with a cruel grin, his sadism on full display. I saw what Schroeder had meant about Edwin's aptitude for Death Camp guard duty: one could see him in a black uniform with SS cap and swastika armband, looming over some terrified captive of the

Third Reich's Aryan racial theory, set to apply torture for an inter-
rogation whose point was not intelligence-gathering but slow suffering inflicted for the sole aim of attaining a murderous,
screaming finale.

He reached out, grabbed up Greta's hand, dragged her struggling out of the chair, pulled her laughing and protesting to a
couch in the corner of the room, and flung her down. He looked at
me. "To hell with you!" he said, "I want the blondie for myself."

"Oh my God!" Schroeder muttered. He turned to me. "I'd better get him out of here."

He lumbered over to Edwin who had pinned Greta to the sofa
with a knee, leaned over her like some silent film villain poised to
do something monstrous, his hand fumbling at his fly. Schroeder's
voice trembled as he tried to reason with him. I quit the room. On
the way out, I noted that Edwin's wife, Trude, stood watching all
this with a glassine stare. We exchanged a quick look. Strangely, I
saw no pain there, no hurt; saw . . . could it be . . . even hints of
masochistic pleasure?

In his office the director and his staff sat quietly with green
beer bottles in hand.

"Look . . ." I began.

The director smiled. "It's all right, Nathan. We'll see that they
leave without incident."

The other staffers studied my face with new interest.

"You certainly travel in unusual circles," said the director.
"But then, this is the writer's privilege, no? It's no doubt one reason why your books are so interesting."

I was prepared to protest that they weren't my friends but
decided not to. Why get Schroeder into trouble for bringing them?
What would that prove? That I'm clean, he's dirty? We're all dirty.
We're all filthy as hell, every one of us. To be human is to excrete
filth, behave filthily. That's why the rare individual who decides to
quit the toilet bowl, climb out, escape, is dangerous, needs to be
put down, flushed. The rest of us slog along the porcelain for as
long as we can until the death flush spins us down the drain to

death; we slog through the shit dumped upon our head by the big pimply ass of circumstance and call this living.

"Yes," I said, unable to meet his eyes. "I guess it's what we writers do." I hated the words even as I spoke them.

His cheek cocked in a sarcastic half-smile. "Yes, well . . ." he said.

Zurich

Chapter 15

Bored, I went to Zurich. Whores now ruled my thoughts. I hoped to anonymously regain, with a Zurich Pole, Czech, Russian, or some exotic mix thereof, a smidgen of the potency I had lost to the Berlin Ukrainian. A website advised that blonde Eastern Europeans were widely available in the city where James Joyce had completed the composition of *Ulysses*.

In the morning I first went to the Irishman's grave. It was in a tidy little cemetery on an elevated bluff where a bronze sculpture of the novelist sat leaning grandly on his ashplant. A small stone bench was provided for personal reflection. I tried to muse on the master's works but couldn't find a single thought to merit his shrine. Instead, I languidly daydreamed about obtaining a whore, fantasized about soft curves framed by lipstick-red lingerie. Flipping open my cell phone, I scrolled through downloaded amateur snapshots of blow jobs and fucks. Particularly obsessed with creamy thighs banded by garters, I grew hard, even while amazed and disgusted to realize how suburban my libido truly is.

But then, wasn't Joyce himself also preoccupied with brothels? He paid frequent drunken visits to them in the company of Italo Svevo, author of *Confessions of Zeno*, who would wheel Joyce home, soused and singing at the top of his lungs, in a borrowed baby tram. But if Joyce's take on loose sex seemed like some sort of holy humanistic emanation from a grand metaphysical intellect, mine ran more along the lines of a Bronx cabby beating off at curbside behind the wheel.

And over there, just a catacomb away from Joyce's resting place, stood the grave of Elias Canetti, an author of less eminence but, still, a sacred monster in his own right. Evidently, the two disliked each other intensely. That their coffins should point to each other for all eternity must have been some local Zuricher's notion of a joke, as was the naming of two streets after the writers that exactly join to form an intersection in an upscale residential district. Leave it to the Swiss to play tricks on the dead. It is for such reasons that, despite their canniness with banks, the Swiss are commonly thought of, overall, as moronic blockheads in lederhosen tinkering with cuckoo clocks, hoarding art and gold stolen by Nazis from gassed Jews, and yodeling joyously on climbs through icy gorges.

After paying my spermy tribute to Joyce, I hopped a cab across town to the Langstrasse, the red-light district—a lurid arcade of faux sixties-free-love psychedelic barrooms and hookah head-shops, Turkish fast food kiosks, sleazy-hooker lingerie boutiques, Middle Eastern falafel joints, and strip clubs. On the sidewalks whores with hiked skirts sat handcuffed behind grim Swiss police-men who stood around talking with self-important airs as though they had captured some big game prey and not a bedraggled group of poor women forced to sell their bodies to survive. Patrol cars with slow revolving blue lights cruised up and down. Not all the whores were swept up in the dragnet, just enough to send a mes-sage. Brothel prostitution is legal in Zurich but not streetwalking. In typical Swiss fashion, as with their banking, hooking is tightly regulated but with unspoken uncodified loopholes. Normally, I'd been told, unregistered trade can play on back streets so long as it's done at night after, say, 10 p.m., when most tourists are indoors and the only ones out cruising under cover of darkness are unsa-vory lechers. So long as the whores remain in shadow on side streets off the main drag, and transactions take place out of sight, *alles gut*. But these desperate girls on the sidewalk had braved their self-interest to make a badly needed franc in broad daylight, a roulette turn on a jailhouse wheel, and now they had turned up losers. Naturally, Johns get off scot-free with a scare. Under one awning three scantily-clad whores who had escaped the dragnet huddled shivering. A gust of cold air rose. The streets were deserted. An Eastern European blonde with a pockmarked face but otherwise not bad-looking, with long slender legs strapped into high-heeled sandals and with high pert breasts in a tight pink halter bearing the image of Bugs Bunny wryly eating a carrot, scurried down the road to avoid a patrol, and as she passed our eyes met, briefly, and her face queried, "So?"

I slowed my feet at the other side of the street, looked at her. She glanced back at me. I nodded. She motioned with her head that I should follow. She cut down a side street, ran up a short flight of steps into a decrepit brown three-story building. I caught up, paused at the doorway, peered in, and saw her there, waiting in the gloom. I entered. She turned and placed a key into a lock, turned the tumbler, pushed open the cheaply-painted brown door bearing the number 3.

I entered a small room painted blue with a single bed, a table, two chairs, and department store bags filled with clothes, especially shoes, some still bearing price tags, and other items spilling out, wigs and scarves and nylons all a tangle. The windowsill doubled as a sideboard on which lay, on a sheet of newspapers scattered with crumbs, a knife, a loaf of bread, a jar of jam, and a shapeless lump of rancid butter turning dark yellow on a caked and crumpled sheet of wax paper. There was no refrigerator, no bathroom. The water closet must have been out in the hall. On a small black wooden box was a cheap lamp, the kind sold in discount stores, a pair of earrings, and the framed photograph of man and child. She turned the picture face down.

"You live here?"

"American?"

"American-Israeli. Your English . . . a nice surprise. You are Polish?"

She nodded. "From Warsaw. I speak a little English."

"So, do you live here?"

She looked away, bored. I told her my name. She gave me hers: "Marta." The way she said it, I could tell she had just made it up. I felt a stab of sadness at that. She didn't trust me. Understandable. Her circumstance fascinated me. I am always amazed to learn of just how desperate people can become, the kinds of things they do to survive. Still, I felt a touch disappointed. What did I expect? Why did I always come bearing expectations to those least able or willing to fulfill them?

Matter-of-factly, she began to undress. I did too. It was strange. Just moments ago, we were rushing past each other on a police-swept street, and were now in a room disrobing. I leaned over, tried to kiss her. A stiff forefinger intruded. "No. Not on the mouth. Never on the mouth. You can't kiss a whore on the mouth." A universal rule, it seemed: Like Lena, whores don't kiss.

We sat on the bed.

"I need a condom," I said. "I don't have one with me."

She smiled. "You don't have one?"

"No," I said. "I don't really like them."

"We can do things that don't need a condom."

"Like what?"

She leaned over my lap, took me in her mouth. I grew hard instantly. Her blonde hair, her smooth white slender body, her breasts, large and firm with pronounced nipples, her voice, her manicured green fingernails and toes, most of all, her sly glance—all worked for me and I lay back, relaxed, let her perform her stuff. I was in the hands—or mouth, as it were—of a pro. The fraught depredations and failures with Lena in Berlin vanished as "Marta" switched to hand motions so delicious that I grunted and ran a finger along the silken back of her ear.

Then she went to both hand and mouth combined, her cupping fingers gently squeezing and urging my testicles to give forth sap which rose shuddering goldenly all through me, and my back arched, and buttocks lifted from the bed; the hand strokes stopped, and just her warm clasping mouth was bobbing now as her lips bore down possessively, insistently, and with a grunt I approved, grabbed a fistful of blondness and rose up on one elbow, gravely watching as her mouth sucked at me, worked me to explosive pitch and then jumped off, let my pole quiver in the air, burning red, seeping drops, her sly watchful eyes narrowing wickedly until I was in an agony of anticipation. Then, her mouth closed over me with what seemed like genuine care and sweetly pumped out every last pent up ecstatic drop stored in there after months of nerve-shattering famine and death wishes with Lena. Spent, I lay there with the bedding's strange musty smell in my nose, thinking with almost mystical clarity of bed bugs.

"Do you have bed bugs?" I asked with a terrified quiver.

She frowned. "What?"

"Nothing. I'm sorry. A stupid question. I think I'm a little delirious. That was amazing."

She sat up with a look of disgust, put on clothes. I dressed too.

"That will be sixty francs," she said.

I gave it to her.

"Do I have to go right at this moment?" I looked at the window, said, "I think I see rain. And the cops are still out there."

Her face grew blank. She shrugged. "Sit. I have nothing to offer."

I sat but could not exactly make myself comfortable. I regretted my imbecilic question, felt like an idiot. I looked around, saw everything sharply, though the sense of almost mystical clarity was quickly wearing off. The room was small and with what business we had had in it concluded took on the suffocating emptiness of a kind of sexual limbo unfit for more than brief quarter-hour stays. She bent to her bags, moved around a few things. She looked straight at me, face flushed from the exertion of bending. She squatted. Her legs were quite muscular. There was a package of cigarettes on the floor. She must have dropped them. The package showed the image of a steamship bearing down on you, prow-first, its funnel trailing a large white plume of smoke.

"I think you dropped something else over there," I said, pointing to a hairbrush on the floor. She looked. At that moment came a loud knock on the door. She opened. A man's voice. She replied. A large brutal face with buzz-cut hair and broken nose thrust itself into the room, looked me over, and withdrew. More talk. She shut the door.

"You have to go," she said.

"Now?"

"Yes."

"But it's still raining."

"He wants you to leave now."

"And who is he?"

She stared. "Look. Don't be stupid. You know who he is. You know where you are. Do yourself a favor and go."

I rose. "One question, please."

"What?"

"Before he came you let me stay . . ."

"I can't work with the cops on the street. It didn't matter if you go or stay. . ."

"But, is there some part of you . . . that let me stay . . . because you like me?"

She produced a cigarette from the steamship packet, put it in her mouth, conjured a lighter from thin air, lit up, and exhaled. "Look, you saw who he is. Go. Now."

"The two in the picture. The photograph. Who are they?"

She stared hard at me. A tremor of emotion passed over her face. "My son," she said. "My son and my husband."

"And, where are they?"

"Why do you ask this?"

"Just curious."

"They are in Gdansk," she said.

Suddenly, her eyes moistened. "No, they are not in Gdansk. Dead," she said. "They are dead. Now, will you go? He is out there. If he comes back here a second time, he might hurt us both."

I left.

Salzburg

Chapter 16

With Gerhardt, I made a second public appearance sponsored by the City of Salzburg in a local lecture hall. The audience sat grimly as we bantered back and forth. More books sold. But I left feeling somewhat hollow. So did Gerhardt, I venture to say. You sit in a tourist town on a cool summer night, talking to sunburned Austrians in summer fur wraps and Lodenfrey blazers about the Holocaust and the whole thing makes you want to jump from a fatal height.

My one productive contribution to that chat was the moment I declared myself "sick of literature, of all that bullshit."

Gerhardt chuckled, understood. But the audience of well-heeled literati and academics gawked, horrified; couldn't bear to think that perhaps they themselves embodied what I meant, the tyranny of their politically-correct scrutiny, the monotony of their preoccupations, the inhibiting wall they present, a solid phalanx of blank-faced mediocrity, the blandness of their purchases, the predictability of their comments, the triumph of their smug brainwashed middle-brow sensibility. Not a few of them, I'm sure, nurtured on Foucault and Derrida, had come because the press had placed above my curly black hair a warning sign that read, "WARNING! Subversive Yid!" They had come to watch the Hebraic King Kong rage under Klieg lights.

Gerhardt offered to drive me back to Innsbruck from which I was to train it back to Zurich. Along the way we decided to stop off at Mauthausen Concentration Camp. We walked up a rolling windy green expanse and entered through the gates of an immense stone fortress of unspeakable agonies, two tiny figures in a dream.

To our amazement, we found, rimmed with the rusted fossils of electric barbed wire, a high stone wall bearing plaques commemorating the torture and murder of victims, hailing, incredibly, from Cuba, China, Russia, France, England, Poland, Mexico, and so on—a veritable Pequod of inconceivable brutality sailing into oblivion under the captaincies of sadistic fiends. As we wandered with bleak, blank faces through the prisoners' threadbare quarters and washrooms, I noticed on my face—glimpsed in a lavatory mirror that once held captive reflections—a small, almost indiscernible smile of sardonic confirmation that such inhumanity does in fact exist; for I hold, always have, that human civilization—with the exception of the Jews—is completely rotten to the core, and I always sport that little smile as though expecting only the worst. Yet, I felt something more, though what precisely I couldn't say. I don't know what Gerhardt felt. Didn't ask. I sensed that like me he, too, must have felt as though we were trespassing on some planet where humans were unwelcome. Neither of us spoke. We only glanced now and then at each other blankly. We moved from room to room like aimless shadows.

We wandered into a museum displaying the meagerest of items, yet each powerfully suggested the magnitude of the crimes that had been committed here: for instance, a striped cap worn when the prisoners stood on the parade grounds for endless hours in subzero temperatures, donning and removing the caps as some camp guard shrieked, "Caps on! Caps off! Caps on! Caps off!" Or a single large stone such as prisoners carried on their shoulders from the quarry up the "Stairs of Death." Or a tin cup and spoon, totems of programmatic starvation.

There was a display of camp badges and their designations. Gerhardt and I tried to identify which of these we would be likely to wear. His was "Reborn Lapsed Catholic"; mine was "Jewish Troublemaker." In the next exhibit was a whipping table, a whip, and illustrations of various tortures and beatings administered at Mauthausen. Then: crematoria. I have also stood, on a previous book tour, before the ovens of Dachau. There is nothing one can say: a wall descends. What is there to imagine? Screaming disbelief as one is inserted alive, as was sometimes the case, into the white-hot inferno?

One's journey on earth ended here, in this iron oven, reduced to ash among the remains of strangers, yourself a stranger, your killers strangers to you, on this strange hilltop of meaningless and needless horror, after having been worked near to death in the performance of labors whose only purpose was to kill you, dying here in ferocious agony, near the town of Mauthausen whose inhabitants, had you attempted to escape, would have helped track you down with even greater zeal than the camp guards. "Hunting the Rabbit" they called it. They got out the dogs, the rifles, the little Tyrolean caps with grand feathers trailing like a steamship's plume and maniacally chased you, huffing up hill and down dale, while you, a scarecrow in striped pajamas, your feet bound in rags, stumbled through the black woods with baying hounds on your scent. What did that feel like? Where was your mother then, your brother or sister or wife or children? Where were your friends? They too endured the unendurable. They too were slaughtered. You were alone. So alone. The only ones who knew of your existence were the killers who ordered the grave that you dug for yourself when they caught you. I wondered if anyone ever made it out of Mauthausen? Unlikely. As I stood there ruminating, Gerhardt snapped pictures of me peering down at the oven's grate, looking pensive.

As if to answer any questions about escape, the very next exhibit displayed prisoners photographed while dying on the electrified fence in a variety of absurdly graceful and acrobatic postures: committing suicide by hurling themselves onto the wire, attempting escape, suspended upside down, stretched along the fence like a moonstruck dreamer, dangling from the fencepost like a marionette from a single arm, or kneeled over it like a supplicating Buddhist. All held me mesmerized. In one, the gape-mouthed prisoner lies perfectly limp in a bed of mud with just one outstretched arm elegantly draped along the wire, pointing upward, as if in casual accusation of God. In another, a man wrapped in the wires appears to be lying on a summertime hammock rather than frying to death on the electrified fence surrounding Mauthausen Concentration Camp, just a stone's throw, a really pleasant drive, from the gay cafés and brothels of Salzburg. In another photograph, a man has both hands pinned by the current's shock to the electrode-studded fence post and he looks like an athlete scoring in some fierce competition against devilish opponents rather than some nameless unfortunate who was kidnapped by uniformed state-sanctioned lunatics and taken to a plein air torture chamber, who in trying to escape died hellishly under a blue sky, in a strange country, among homicidal sadists and their endless supply of barely-living victims.

At the top of the "Stairs of Death" which the prisoners mounted in perfectly kept ranks under a constant rain of blows from whips and clubs, each prisoner shouldering an impossibly heavy stone, the SS would, just for kicks, shove the top row of prisoners backwards, causing a lethal avalanche of prisoners and rocks, necks breaking, arms snapping, legs, backs, skulls crushed. Those too injured to stand back up immediately were shot, the corpses removed to some nameless pit for burial and the less injured forced to stand once more in perfect ranks and again begin the torturous climb with a stone on the shoulder and this went on from dawn to dusk.

Those who made it to the top were sometimes led fifty feet away to the cliff's edge, near the foot of which sat picnicking SS with lunches of sandwiches, roast chicken, wine. This amusement was known as "The Parachutists," a favorite with camp administrators. Standing one behind the other, on signal the man behind must push the man in front. Of course, the first one at the cliff's edge went right over and the "Parachutist" fell screaming to his death. The watching SS applauded and cheered. Then, the next, and the next, and so on.

"I tried," said Gerhardt weakly, when we got back into the car and drove off in numb silence "to imagine you there."

"And could you?

"Yes," he said.

"And could you imagine yourself there?"

"Yes, but I will try not to think about this."

Chapter 17

I'm falling away from the motions of life, of history, of all that I have known, the need to eat, breathe, look at art, read, socialize, practice spiritual self-healing exercises, play the lottery. I cannot even bring myself to replace my worn, frayed clothes with new ones or have a doctor look me over; sunk as I am into a weary torpor of self-neglect punctuated by a burning rectal throb that I must remind myself is not hemorrhoids, no, but caused by—I failed to mention this—her ferret-eyed insistence upon sticking her sharp-nailed fingers up my bun as she sucks on my by-now incredibly sore nipple. And, for all I know, the pain is becoming ass cancer, a truly horrible way to go; the symptoms include dark red or black blood in the bowl, acute constipation cramps, diarrhea, long thin pencil-like stools, fatigue, weakness, abdominal discomfort, bloating, and unexplained weight loss, all of which I've suffered since meeting Lena.

Once, one of her false fingernails broke off in my ass and was stuck up there for two whole weeks. When I crapped it out, she shoved me off the toilet, found the acrylic tip imbedded in a turd, fished it out like an Atlantis arisen from my bloody ass, and kept it as a souvenir, something to remind her of me when she is cavorting in a jungle resort with burglarizing monkeys, being mounted by her tennis-bum philosophizing lover, Rolf, ecstatically moaning amid the toucans and papaya.

All I want is to wake up in the world as it was before her, to return to that by-now-mythical time when I could get it up with anyone and the word Viagra never once entered my thoughts. I am now hurtling from somewhere to nowhere, feeling and seeing Lena's face before me, fawn-eyed, wan, with long silken brown hair that tumbles around her slender shoulders, a nineteenth-century woman with ruthless twenty-first-century values and a libido like an adulterous nymphomaniacal Silicon Valley sales rep.

My insatiable need to fuck her has taken me to the lowest possible depths, yet I am determined to love her properly, as once I knew how to, rock hard, in the saddle, in charge, working her into raptures, delivering swift forceful rhythmic strokes or else long loving flourishes and expressive dips, sucking a single breast on and on, pinching the other nipple firmly between thumb and forefinger, kissing her ear, her neck, withdrawing my sword of light, withholding until she begs, then reinserting slowly, to feel the length and width occupy her and move in slow rotations, then to withdraw and repeat. But now during panicked encounters she shoves me off, rolls atop, gropes and grabs my dick against my will. I go flaccid; it just hangs there shrunken like a spoiled brown banana until she moves off, stretches out, does something with her hand to make it semi-hard, pretends to be pliant, then suddenly jumps aboard for a solo rodeo romp that leaves me feeling fiercely desperate for human connection, so empty I could weep. Still, I exist only for her Skyped face to cling to, gaze at; I nuzzle the screen with my nose like a subordinated cat.

I need her love right now! Yet, though I turn ravenous deflowering eyes on hot young Millennials, my stare is Chaplanesque, doleful, for I am a drowning choking jester tainted by the certainty that there's no longer any chance to have such soft-skinned women, rosy in their twenties, with their pert firm little breasts and plush lips, without paying a full price measured in harrowing indignities. To them I am, after all, just some gray alien corpse of a lusting codger, a sugar daddy good only for whatever money or opportunities I may offer. I offer none. Besides, how truly awful after rolling all night in the sack with a young wench to witness in her eyes, come morning, her sickened realization of just how physically trashed I really am, how revolted she truly feels.

Twelve years younger than I, Lena's relative youth is her trump card and she plays it like a sharpie. My inexhaustible yearning has made her pitiless. She imagines that she owns my cock. Which, horribly, she does.

The Berlin Woman

She yanks at the belt of fat banding my waist, lectures me on my small, barely visible bald patch, grabs at my pectorals declaring them to be female, and sucks hungrily at my nipples like a nursling, swearing that my "man-breasts," which once could bench press four hundred and twenty-five pounds without a spotter, remind her of her mother's teats.

I know that she means well by this cruel way of showing love, because afterwards, postcoitus, like a child, she softly enfolds herself in my every crevice, inviting me to nurse her. She wants my dick to stand and yet to fail. Having sex with me, she experiences a sudden infancy. Indeed, she has made me into her mother. After all, a mother does not want to fuck her daughter: instead, I should offer her a breast.

But I have no wish to rebirth her. I want to penetrate her with a retributive sense of agency for how she makes me feel during our brief cataclysmic rendezvous. And as she must know, the sensation of her lips gnawing on my nipple I find traumatically disagreeable. This faux breast-feeding shit is a royal pain in the tit. Occasionally, she bites, which makes my dick flail and hide, shrunk to such near-invisibility that to find it I must dislodge it like a wedged cork. The quagmire of shame has become my new normal. Yet part of me wants to nurture her, if that is what she needs, and I do, in our brief trysts, to the best of my ability, by letting her suck on my pecs, and trying to be maternal.

But since meeting her I have started awakening at night, to stand shirtless as Putin before hotel bathroom mirrors, examining the teeth marks she's left, cupping my chest, lifting my pecs to imagine myself in a bra, worried that I need some kind of man-bra, if such a thing exists. Already, I've wasted two whole afternoons Googling "man breasts," scanning websites with pastel-colored fonts, to see if my chest qualifies. It doesn't, not by a long shot. Yet, after a lifetime of pushups and weight training, football and combat infantry, I, who once was a man's man, have now become a woman's mother.

I am only paraphrasing my conscious thoughts because, with Lena, one day there's kindness, the next day none. One day you live in a democracy, until you live in a dictatorship. You never think that Tyranny will happen and then it is as though Democracy, Freedom, had never been.

Write a book? I can't imagine it. A deep weariness descends. A disgust with possibilities. Hasn't this all been done before? Before and after the Holocaust haven't an endless number of books, histories, memoirs, fragmented accounts, filmed testimonies, and documentaries streamed forth? Twenty-five years after Auschwitz, in the 1970s, weren't Jewish studies departments launched with chairs endowed by guilty American Jewish billionaires whose families had escaped the slaughter; and how many unctuous readings by poets and authors were sponsored by this foundation or that trust fund, attended by upright and well-mannered sophisticates and intellectuals of the upper-middle class academic set, invigorated by tasteful high-minded Holocaust prose that somehow succeeded to tippy toe around the Unthinkable, make palatable a Holocaust over which panel discussions raged and magazine articles frothed and moaned by the thousands and lots of careers were launched, mine included, and monies were made and households subsidized and classrooms filled and refilled and degrees in Holocaust studies handed out; yet somehow the terror of the mothers and children rounded up during the Warsaw Ghetto revolt and thrown alive into the fires of Treblinka were never quite looked at in detail, or at all. An unsparing truthful book like Tadeusz Borowski's *This Way for The Gas, Ladies and Gentlemen*, was rarely taught or even mentioned; nor was Leon Wells's *Janowska Road*. Instead, as Yehudi Menuhin's violin played, we fed the world a soulful pablum of Elie Wiesel and Steve Spielberg. Synagogue congregants assembled to watch *Schindler's List*, followed by catered lunch in the Sam and Marilyn Gross Community Hall. Such fare became the height of Holocaust tribute. And there were night table readings from the comic book *Maus* with a sneak raid on the fridge for a dish of Ben and Jerry's to palliate the aggravation.

The ghost of the dead arose to torment my heart even as History was preparing to tear my flesh. Write a book? What would be the point? The next killers will find me anyway. And what of the dead? What of their ghosts? By what Ouija board can they be contacted? We don't even know their names.

The annihilation of the Jews of Europe sparked a quest for answers to something for which none were possible. We made a cult of asking questions, when all along the answer was quite simple: in the twentieth century, during the Holocaust, we Jews learned that God is not enough; that without a state, without an army, without a government of our own, we are doomed to certain annihilation. What could be simpler? All our questions had been answered, horribly, six million times over. But the questioning went on and on, and soon became a well-endowed industry. How could this annihilation have happened, we asked, not really wanting to know, since the answer stared us squarely in the face: a once-martial people had in exile become defenseless and had no way to rearm. Nonetheless, we proceeded to explain everything but the inexplicable thing that had happened, turning academic scholarship into a new form of liturgical summons, a ceaseless public ceremonial wake pandering to the populace and cross-fertilizing industrialized mass murder with postmodern references to everything from comic books to Hollywood, so that now even the most well-intended have so completely lost their way that there is no way back. Israel was the answer—but no, we had to punch holes in that too, tear ourselves apart with insipid though agonizing moral quandaries that paid no heed to that over which we agonized. All along the answer stared us in the face; one need only look at a photograph of any scarecrow in striped pajamas, or better yet, the gaping vacant stare of a gassed corpse. But the answer was never good enough for those who had not endured such torments. They required the intellectual imprimatur of theories spawned by Foucault, Derrida, Lacan, Marx, and the YHWH of all neatly ensconced Jewish intellectuals: Walter Benjamin, despite that he died in a Twilight Zone suicide, suspended between the fascist borders of Franco's Spain and Péain's France. His death should have provided a clue. But it did not. For among today's high IQ elite survival is not only no longer prized but has been, at depth, displaced by the Kafkaesque notion of a "posthuman world," in which Mother Earth rids herself of humanity altogether. Deep in his or her heart every modern Jewish Walter Benjaminesque foe of Israel's ironclad military solution to such imponderables as Jewish annihilation is a pitiless nihilist besotted with theory, divorced from reality, and incapable of grasping Life with both hands and producing something more than a dense and unreadable thesis.

Culture has waged its own meritless war against Reality. How many art exhibits display the same kitsch barbed-wire impressionistic diorama blowups of a Nazi aiming his rifle at a naked Jewish mother clutching her naked child to her breasts, to a point where the image means nothing? How many symphonies with weeping chorales and harrowing oboes and alarmed flutes have played to somber sold-out crowds in diamonds and furs? How many sentimental and irrelevant Spielbergesque Holo-flicks win prizes at Cannes and Sundance, as though awards and not the unthinkable truth were the point, and from the hallowed halls of Hollywood to the shores of Burbank always the same trembling violin film score accompanies the victims, as if they had perished in the smothering bosoms of wheedling mothers to the strains of Yehudi Menuhin and had not gone naked screaming shitting themselves and utterly abandoned into the gas chamber and fiery pit? And how many museums need to be erected—architectural glories by the finest talents *gelt* could buy—to celebrate universalized victimization or provide Instagram opportunities for Shoah tourists? How many times is the Holocaust invoked for just about any controversy from gun control to fracking; or, from stem cell research to climate change?

Despite all of this, or because of it, the death of six million Jews changed nothing; went the way of last year's losing Oscar nominees; became, like all else, just so much filler content for the Internet, though it quickly lost its digital appeal, too, dropped way down the probability scale of subjects likely to "go global" or earn on Twitter a volume of six-, five-, or even four-digit responses. And no less than for Hitler or Stalin, spreading distrust of Jews is now a very useful political tool for both the American Right and the Left, Democrats and Republicans, while alt-right "cleverism" uses hatred of Jews to promote white Aryan supremacy, and the Far Left, weirdly, embraces the anti-Semitic fundamentalist propaganda of Hamas, Hezbollah, or even the Black Muslims to inflame their Marxist base.

So, my mother's survival of mind-numbing horror was pointless, as if Auschwitz, Buchenwald, Treblinka, Dachau, had never occurred. Even Holocaust deniers are becoming the frequent subject of independent films with indignant determined heroes desperate to prove deniers wrong, as if it mattered to anyone but an increasingly marginalized handful. Now there was something that anyone could be: not deniers, but Holocaust forgetters. Sixty percent of polled American teens have never heard of Auschwitz. It doesn't take a prophet to grasp that, against a gathering storm of jihadists, alt-right fanatics, and anti-Zionist BDSers, words and even images would have no impact on anything whatsoever, nor would the personal accounts of authentic survivors, those quaint relics stammering in their broken English in Spielberg-funded videos about horrors that no longer seem horrible, since everyone living face-down in smart phones and nurtured by ISIS snuff has become incapable of caring.

And anyway, after all, it happened so long ago—it's practically prehistoric history! Hitler, Stalin, Mussolini, Goering, Heydrich, Himmler—such names carry as much weighty irrelevance as Vlad the Impaler and Atilla the Hun. The Left has bemoaned the Holocaust but hated Israel. The Right has supported Israel but hated the Jews. Thanks to the Internet, the world is drowning in untruths. Every asshole with a laptop can be an impresario seer. The Great God Digital has won! Talking heads and opinionated malcontents are its anointed führers and only the most spectacularly brutal images get emojied enough times to win social media cache: an Isis-crucified child earned a mere 'Ugh!' A beheaded Japanese journalist got 'Liked.' A Jordanian pilot burned alive in a cage won an OMG and did one lap around the nightly news programs. These things were done to stun you into posting a response.

Images of Holocaust atrocities now appear to be as trite as Donald Duck, Mickey Mouse, or Betty Boop. Gas chambers? Who gives a fuck? No one.

Sometimes, when conscience moved the hive mind, when a particularly grisly Holocaustal image popped up on Facebook, typical comments were:

"No!"

"Yikes!"

"The Bastards!"

"Another American CIA ploy to trick us to put boots on foreign soil!"

"Israel committed the Holocaust! Gas chambers were an Israeli invention! It's so obvious!"

"Just like that Tarantino flick . . . what's the title? Hey guys, need help here. Anyone???"

"Inglourious Basterds, moron!"

Never in my life had I thought to see such a day. Paralyzed, instead of writing I wake into a world that has become, to me, unknowable, futureless, a pit whose dimensions measure thirty feet by fifty feet by ten feet of field dirt at the bottom of which Lena and I embrace, sardine-stacked atop corpses, our globe-shaped white buttocks kissed by Polish winds.

I want only to sleep for I am tired of normalization of the unthinkable, the mounting obscenity against me. Of course, Lena wants to escape to some jungle with Rolf. Who can blame her? Of course, she chooses to see Trump and Putin as saviors rather than the grotesque and lethal monsters that they are. Reality is so unbearable! Why not concoct a fairy tale, pretend to be Alice swallowed up by a children's-book world of puzzling and curious opposites and contradictions rather than the murderous marching ground of the bloody jackboot?

But, my dear Alice, whether you are Jewish or black or gay or trans or a woman (or whatever you are that has inspired others to hate you), the dead follow. They are always just one step behind. The gassed Jews, the raped and slain women, the kidnapped children, the whipped and lynched enslaved blacks, the tortured and burned witches, the queers thrown by true believers from Middle Eastern roofs, follow in the millions upon millions, right behind you, reminding you of their persecutions everywhere you go.

Vienna

Chapter 18

The next morning Schroeder Skyped. Online, his face was florid; he wore his silver-rimmed glasses, beige sports jacket, pinstriped black shirt—a kind of uniform for him. From the background I guessed him to be in a hotel somewhere.

"Schroeder," is all I said.

He studied my face on his screen. "You didn't sleep?"

"Not well."

"Lena?"

I nodded. Of course, he knew. Better even than I knew.

"Listen," he said. "I don't tell you how to live your life, yes? But she is so crazy. She will make you sick. You don't look well. A little sick."

"Not a little," I said. "More than a little."

"Listen. You remember I told you about that reading in Vienna?"

I nodded. "I do."

"They want you. They pay 650 euros plus train and hotel. The usual. I already have you booked in the hotel. Buy the train ticket and they will reimburse you in their office when you arrive."

"When is this for?"

"Tomorrow night. You must leave today. I have you in Vienna for one night. Then, you go on to Berlin and have two nights free before your reading."

"I don't understand. Vienna and Berlin back to back on short notice. There'll be no publicity. No one will come. I won't even be in their fucking calendars."

"You are not the whole bill. Each one had a cancellation. You will be an 'instead of.' You're advertised on the websites. And in Vienna Gerhardt will interview you. It will be billed as 'Onstage Conversation.'"

"You're joking, right? Billed? Billed where? On my behind?"

"Look. Berlin rush-ordered fifty copies of your book, paid for up front. Five-O! It will be a big event."

"How much for Berlin? In euros."

He hesitated. "Only three hundred. The plane tickets. The hotel of course."

"Of course," I said icily.

"I'm sorry about the money. But I said yes . . . look. The book is . . ." He struggled for how to say the next thing.

"Doing shit." I helped him.

"Not that poorly, no," he said sadly. "But not super. You know, here, there are many books about the Holocaust and sometimes those do good but not too many care what happened to your generation, the sons and daughters of the survivors. That's Not Their Problem."

"I'm tired, Schroeder."

"Berlin could change that. Important critics will be in the audience."

"It won't matter. All my books sell poorly. It's no different in America or England. I told you when you bought the rights that you're throwing your money down a hole. I'm a bottomless pit, a wasted time. I apologize. I'm so sorry. To publish me was a miscalculation."

"Do you know why I published you?"

"You thought Holocaust sells."

"No. And not because I want to make up for the fact that my whole fucking family were unrepentant Nazis."

"Because you want to get laid and think that association with me will make you seem attractive?"

"Perhaps there was some of that in my decision, yes. But look, maybe you're not famous like Michael Jackson but some of us here had heard of you, your other books, your crazy adventures, your wars, your bohemian life, your bedroom exploits. We all thought here that you were a Casanova. But now this thing with Lena. Nathan. Forgive me. But you are pathetic."

My face dropped and nodded in shame. "I know."

"I published you, cocksucker, because you are a truly great writer. It is funny that you have all these experiences with women but that is not why some of us here admire you. It is because your writing reminds us that all is not lost, that there is still the possibility of real literature."

"Right. Okay, Schroeder, you flattering fuck. You sound like when you first approached me about the rights to the book. Same smooth line. But you and I know I'm a lost cause."

"No! No! I disagree! It just needs time. You will see . . ."

"Every publisher I've ever had said those exact same words to me."

"Have hope," said Schroeder.

"No," I replied. "I refuse hope."

"One more thing. You will go back to America after Berlin, yes? It is the last booking. I have arranged your flight. I will email you a ticket."

"Keep your ticket. I'm not going back. I've got savings. I'll book my own flight if and when I'm ready. I have plenty of air miles to spend."

"But what will you do?"

"I don't know," I said. "I feel lost. Maybe I'll get more lost. Maybe for good."

"The woman has driven you bat shit."

"No. I can't blame Lena. It's not her. Well, maybe a little. But it's more than that. Much more. Will you be in Vienna?"

"Yes."

"Okay. I'll see you there."

The fact was I knew deep down that I could not blame her in any way. It was my choice to be with her. Me putting me in there. Knowing what I did about her which was, actually, quite little and yet going for her anyway. Knowing that I hadn't the emotional capacity to grasp at any level what drove her to make the choices she did, and at the same time, though I could not have said as much, at some level understanding all of her decisions, even those that hurt me the most, even when knowing at some deep monastically altruistic level that reeked sanctimoniously of pity and unwashed piety—and was, likely, just another manifestation of my outright gift for self-delusion—about her coming trip with Rolf and that, at the moment she boarded the plane with him for Cuba or wherever the fuck they were headed, the clock would tick tock and then it would not be long that questions that had haunted me my whole life would be answered with the ironclad certainty of a gunshot.

Berlin

Chapter 19

So, this is the hard part, one that even I have difficulty admitting to: that it was I and no other out there in Berlin's night streets behind the central railway station where in full public view, with plenty of the proverbial train station whores about, I tried to purchase a small-caliber handgun off of one or another seedy Serb, Montenegrin, Ghanian, or Turk who loitered about the high arched gates—men with an air of desolation who were practiced in low-level profitless crimes—suspicious types on whom any frisking policeman would be almost certain to find something worth his while, at the very least, a minor felony count. But the cops didn't bother with these small fry—and of those whom I approached none seemed to have the least idea of how to obtain, under the table, a cheap silver-plated .22, which was a lie. All of them knew. They just didn't trust me.

As a last resort I stopped a pair of quite hostile Africans with deep ceremonial scars scoring their cheeks who glared with resentful suspicion as I tried to explain by hand gestures and wild facial expressions my willingness to pay as much as 300 euros for a cheap gat, for I only needed to fire off one shot—just your basic cheap death tool to terminate my hopeless excuse for a life.

My idea was to ring her up at an hour when I knew she'd be home alone, step across the threshold, smile as though on some casual drop-in visit, sit and chitchat—though by now her implacable instincts would scream danger—and at the right instant talk to her of Panama, wish her a bon voyage, a great suntan. Then suddenly, quite nonchalantly, I'd produce the gun, place it on the table, toy with it as I spoke, her eyes by now wide as she fixed her disdainful attention on it, and explain that for her to see it as something potentially dangerous, a reason for fear, is in fact to err—as I am hopelessly in love with her (she knows that all too well) and there is no possibility that she and I will ever be together on any sort of normal footing. She might look upon the gun as a benign, even a merciful, remedy for deadlocked monumental suffering—such anguish as no human being should ever have to endure. At which point I would, in the plainest, most cliché of gestures, lodge the gun under my chin, utter the words, "Farewell my lovely," and squeeze off a Hemingway.

Rolf's tanned six-pack had won. In my mind, I could not shake the thought of his flabby washboard crushing her belly-sweetness, his immense sunburned, chai-flavored horse cock sliding in and out between her lovely Eastern European thighs, her legs hoisted in his arms, flip flops pressed against the thatched ceiling, his clenched muscular ass ramming home, Othello's white ewe tupped by a Viking dwarf in Birkenstocks.

But I could not find the gun or some quick means to execute my blood-soaked advertisement for self-cancellation. I have always had a buckling fear of heights, such that I won't even dare peer out the window of a skyscraper office or over the edge of my own sixth-floor San Francisco apartment's balcony (though oddly I don't mind traversing continents in planes). I feel averse to drowning or any form of choking death, for as a child I quite regularly suffered from severe asthma attacks like a fish on a boat deck sucking air. Also, I have inherited my grandmother's pouchy stomach, a bit wide at the base, never quite muscular, cursed by a touch of fat if you will. Over and over it recurs like some PTSD reflexive recollection of a terrorist attack how, as we lay together, Lena had grabbed the belt around my navel, said, "You must lose this . . . do sit-ups. I don't go with fat men!"

"So I can have abs like Rolf?"

She smiled nervously. "Yes."

"So that when you look at me you won't think of him."

"No. So that after this I will want to think of you. Right now, your body makes me sick."

But I felt sure that, sit-ups or not, Lena thought of me too little to divert her from Panama.

It occurred to me that she did not know where I was or even

how to find me. Even I didn't know. My permanent address was a Jerusalem PO box. Mostly I was on the road, to do book signings, readings, give talks, make radio and television appearances, stay on the move. I was always in demand, in Europe. People wanted to know about the things I had lived through, learn about them from the safety of a bookstore or auditorium seat, or from their own crumb-sprinkled sofa.

I was that guy, the good-looking rostrum artist with an easy-listening voice, dashing sideburns turning gray, and always ready with the right word choice, persuasive, full of novel ideas but who could not, unfortunately, prevent the woman for whom he had waited his whole life from taking off for a three-month jaunt with her stunted Nordic stud.

I wandered in Berlin with a dreadful ache, for there is, after all, no better town on earth in which to feel utterly miserable and lost. Berlin's spectacular hordes of spruce, dynamic-looking folks seeming gaily intent upon proving to some hovering sky-führer that they live with perfect anti-Nazi equanimity—Berlin a super democracy arisen from the crematoria's ashes in the political, economic, and cultural capital of the tottering European Union; determined to prove, most particularly to themselves, that where they work, create, earn, shop, play, and fuck is no longer the nerve center of the most efficiently sadistic murder regime in human history but an earnest and well-meaning Mother Goose nest for hatching the triumphant possibilities of social and economic redemption. All the soot of war's smoke has been water-blasted from Berlin's buildings; all the guilt of the corpse-burning pits scrubbed clean from the cheeks and brows of their well-fed, guiltless children.

A prosperous peace and the leadership of Europe is Germany's punishment for the Holocaust while the Jew's reward for surviving the gas chambers is to defend the Jewish state against ceaseless genocidal war.

Of course, official shame for the Holocaust has been monumented everywhere in Berlin, an epidemic of commissioned contrition: plaques on buildings and even underfoot on the sidewalks, sculptures, exhibits, memorials, renamed streets, a veritable theme park of formalized remorse, so guilefully done that one does not really see it at first, or does but thinks not of the systematic mass murder of six million Jews but instead remarks on the tasteful handling of genocide's commemoration, of how well the horror has been publicly estheticized and formally sanitized. One might even think that in some bizarre way the guilt-inspired artworks were an inverted form of boasting of how many Jews were killed and of the great artistic renaissance that had been made of their demise which is precisely what I thought when faced by a tall tasteful slate-colored form rising from out of the sidewalk, gently twisting skywards and which I learned, upon squinting near-sightedly at a tiny gold-plated plaque, was the work of a young sculptor from Cologne "symbolizing the tragic loss of six million Jews."

That broke the spell. It felt like a boast. "Six million! That's quite a lot!"

Loss? How does one "lose" six million Jews? Funny thing happened to me on the way back from the beer hall. Six million Jews packed in the back of my haycart but, *Gott im Himmel*, by the time I got home, they were gone up in smoke!

The Holocaust memorializations of Germany commemorate "loss" but not murder, gassing, burning, starvation, slave labor, mass execution, rape, beatings, torture, medical experiments, hanging, butchering with axes and crow bars, mass grave executions, and machine gun slaughter. In other words, the chaste memorials are absent the particulars. And though I got the sculpture's subtle crematorium inference, still, none of the actual killing methods at Auschwitz or Buchenwald, Dachau or Treblinka, looked in practice like a slender Brancusi knock-off sculpture wreathing gently into the sky. The smoke of millions of incinerated human bodies was greasy, ashes fallen all about the countryside like fragments of charred clothes fluttering on the wind from a burning tenement.

Hungry, I stopped in at a working-class Turkish eatery. Come nightfall a misty drizzle fell in which I walked along, collar upturned, shoulders hunched, hands pocketed, like the child-slayer in *M*. When the rain stopped the whores came out in their fishnets and high boots—black-haired Turks and blonde Slavs, some spectacularly beautiful, though all with faces stamped by bitterness. I was tempted but refrained; felt no real desire anyway, except for death. Of course, I found myself close to her street, in a district famed for its young gay rent boys, and some of them were out, even propositioned me as I walked past, many no more than fifteen or sixteen, hailing from Albania, spending a few warm months on Berlin streets selling their butts, then bringing the saved cash back home to disperse among family, purchase gifts, and date the girl they left behind with whom they plan someday to wed, have kids.

But then I was standing directly across the street from her building, looking up at its windows, the lights on in there. Proba-bly, she was with Hubert. I sat in a doorway, gazing up at windows that I knew belonged to her private studio, saw her pass briefly by. What should I do? Find a cyber café, Skype-call her? Nearby, the Symphony Café had a pay-by-the-minute PC loaded with Skype. I logged on; she answered, white dots spinning her into an impressionistic swirl that moved, and then jelled as her face, trans-mitted.

"You," she typed, a finger to her lips.

"Yes, me."

She leaned close to the screen, squinted, donned glasses, looked again, not at me but my surroundings. "You're in Symphony," she said. "What are you doing? What is this about?"

"Hubert's home?"

"No. But I can't speak."

"The finger at your lips is for . . . ?"

Tears welled in her eyes. "You called to torture me?"

"I called because I'm three blocks away from you and you should either invite me over or come here."

After an agonizing pause, she said what I most dreaded to hear: "I can't do that now. It's complicated . . ."

My heart froze. "Rolf is there . . ."

"How long are you in Berlin for? We can meet tomorrow."

"He's fucking there! You're fucking him tonight! Hubert is in Austria, to see his parents, isn't he! Rolf is there . . . HEY, Rolf, You cocksucking prick! Do you hear me . . . !"

Quickly, she leaned back, face cold. Her hand moved. The screen died.

I rushed from the café, ran three blocks to her flat, my body enacting some primal mission for the kind of violent retribution that launched a thousand ships at Troy or Jack the Ripper at Whitechapel. Only when I reached the building's front door did I understand that I expected Rolf, like some character in an adulterous slapstick flick, to slip out, hurry down the street, avoid me, whereupon I would snatch him by his scrawny neck, beat him senseless.

But no one came. He was up there, flabby washboard abs and all. Heart pounding, fists clenched, adrenalin flooding me so hard I shivered, I braced to kill, but her windows went dark. I repositioned myself across the street, watched to see if anyone materialized at a curtain, peered out from the impenetrable gloom, but no, she must be lying naked with him now, embracing. I began to sob, stumbled across the street to the doorway, slid down, recessed in shadow, my shoulders shaking, and the Berlin sky lit with strange tints of blue glowing among the gray and silver clouds.

How, I wondered, have I come to be so completely and utterly alone? Abandoned? Brokenhearted? Was I ever a child with hopes? Loved by a mother, relatives, friends? Was there anyone in the world to care what happened to me? To all these, yes. Why then am I pursuing this loveless phantom like an affection-starved orphan?

Because on Skype sometimes she lay down with her tablet propped on a pillow beside her face, and turning sideways looked directly at me, appeared so young and innocently beautiful, lips rosy pink, big melting eyes soft with love, like a fawn.

Come dawn I surrendered my doorway outpost, rose unsteadily to my feet, gazed up hopefully at her windows during which my face assumed a variety of silent-film expressions of hopeless

longing that with a little powder and paint might have drawn
laughs, had they been staged or filmed, had anyone been there to
see or care; but I am one whose worst suffering occurs in a void, a
deep-dish bowl of clear-broth urine-yellow emptiness through
which I float, screaming for help, drowning and rising, thrashing
and sinking, falling in perfect silence, on back streets, along high-
ways, in subway cars or motel rooms, in locales that often I have
no connection to whatsoever, without even the philosophic conso-
lation of a Chaplin, Keaton, or Beckett, to know that one's slapstick grief is at least on view for others to laugh at, and on the long
black road to which I now came, beneath an elevated train track,
stood an endless row of wordless shivering whores, beseeching
silent film-like at oncoming traffic. I had so much pity, for them,
myself. My skin too felt the motherless cold damp; like the hookers my needful flesh stood pitted against heartless love in a soulless city. But unlike them I had nothing to offer, only my heart to
the one person on earth, Lena, who was most meant to have it but
didn't want it or couldn't quite make up her mind if jungle sex
with a midget Viking and a life of loveless safety with an Austrian
Eraserhead were worth trading in for true love with a broke literary drifter, who lived from day to day at the behest of institutional
favor, dependent upon invitations to read, the fees they paid, rev-
enue that could at any moment dry up.

I walked along, pausing to study the whores who gestured for
me to come along. I smiled sadly, shrugged using my best Buster
Keaton imitation, though it felt real enough, unstudied, as though
from an unspliced fragment of black and white reel left on the
cutting room floor of the projection room in my Id, dangling apa-
thetically from the hands of an immense clock overlooking an
abyss in my ego . . .

And then it was nearly dawn, which stank of another's semen
caked on my soulmate's thighs; dawn that broke futilely against
those big empty impenetrable windows of personal betrayal
behind which she slept as I shuffled exhausted through a halluci-
nated and sleepless arcade of a city, past snapshot glimpses of the
high-heeled haunches of weary desperate Lili Marlenes and who

like me were walking aimlessly this morning all over Berlin, and when they stopped to wave down cars that passed and slowed with a tired hissing gravel sound of tires before speeding off, the whores stood upright, cursing with hardened faces, looking about, and when they saw me nodded inquiringly. I signaled back my Keaton-esque "no" and the predawn clown degradation parade to Nowhere rolled on. For we are all whores, each one of us out here, everyone alive, everywhere, and also those two up there, behind her windows. Funny how a simple insight like that can sum us all up so handily, with so little persuasion needed for any person who takes a good hard look in the mirror to ask, "Is that true? Am I too?" and hears the lucid whispering voice from back of the mind reply, "Yes."

Chapter 20

Slowly the streets began to fill with digitalized walking carcasses of pharmaceutically benumbed and shopping-mall outfitted proper citizen-whores dressed in drab business outfits of gray and black and beige and navy blue, off to labor in the administrative salt mines and mills of the corporations. And they looked less animated, less hungrily alive than even the street whores. Those whores seemed human; these did not. Those whores showed personality, vivacity, a hunger for life that ran down their disappointed faces like ruined mascara and even the tired ones looked fresh compared to the young brain-dead army marching off to die of stress in their cubicles.

Not a one looked at me, read my face or my overall condition of shattered nerves and broken heart. Not a one caught the imploring look of piteous need for human warmth in my eyes.

The buildings loomed taller and starker as I made my way to the city center. From Lego structures glittering with gold (perhaps smelted out of Jewish teeth) hung huge logo banners in which the word "Deutsche" frequently appeared. Only decades after the Nuremberg torchlight rallies and here they were so damned proud to be Germans! And Germans, Germans everywhere but not a one to talk to about what was breaking my heart. I wanted to shriek, "First you killed my people for no good reason; now when I am in love you ignore me to death!"

A voice, German, from behind said, "Are you all right?" A tremulous female voice spoke English.

I turned. There stood a woman in a salmon-colored one-piece pullover dress with pale green shoes and her hand on the grip of an orange and gray luggage carrier, not quite beautiful though her face radiated gentleness and temperamental compassion.

"No," I said a bit belligerently. "I am not okay."

"Is there something I can do to help you?"

Tears striped my dirty cheeks.

Instinctively, her hand reached out, touched my arm, remained, resting there lightly but firmly, unafraid. I looked down at it. Then, at her face. I saw fear and sympathy wrestle in her eyes.

She said, "You poor man," and, tugging on my sleeve to pull me out of the swelling deathly flood tide of the commuting labor force rising all around us, said, "Here, come . . ."

Like a dog I followed, with unquestioning trust, into an almost deserted café. In one corner a thickset man with a shaved head and a gold earring sat laughing with two worn-out-looking hookers, both bottle blondes, one with pocked face, wearing the standard black tube dress, easy to lift, as needed; the other with good skin, in red vinyl hot pants and open-toed bright red high-heeled platform shoes that displayed a raspberry-colored pedicure. Both wore big hoop earrings, had pouty lipsticked pillow mouths. Each was outfitted head to toe for the impersonal arousal of the male libido. Everything their mothers told them that men want. And their mothers were right.

The bald thug's eyes—clearly, he was their pimp—followed us to our table where we sat ourselves self-consciously, ominously out of place. It felt unsafe in there, as though my bad juju had dragged down this helpful innocent bystander into my hellish orbit. Yet she radiated a lovely light from her innocent face that made her immune from all forms of wrong-doing. Even the pimp-thug, after scrutinizing her carefully, appeared to relax his guard, turned away. About me, I could tell he remained unsure but must have assumed that whatever threat I might somehow pose was neutralized by her company.

A waiter approached, took our order of two coffees, vanished behind a curtain.

"Are you all right?" she asked.

"Yes," I said.

"Are you sure? Your hands . . . look."

They were trembling.

"I don't know," I said, looking away sadly at nothing in particular. "I feel that I am bones knocking around in a skin bag, without any content or purpose. Just a biomorphic engine of ambulatory adaption surviving without reason."

"I'm not sure what that means."

Suddenly, I reached up, touched her cheek. She let me. "You're very nice to help me like this. I like you."

"I like you too," she said, charitably.

At that, I laid my head on the table, closed my eyes, felt her fingers, maternal, in my hair.

"You're very tired. You didn't get much sleep last night? Yes?"

"No," I murmured. "Not very much. I slept in a doorway."

"Oh no!" I heard her say.

"Not for lack of money. But because I was outside the home of the woman I love. Lena. She's not only married but having an affair with another man. The husband was gone last night. The lover was over there."

She did not appear to know what to say to that. It was enough to strike God himself mute. "That is why . . ." I said to no one and everyone and anyone who would listen, "That is why . . ." but I couldn't think of how to finish the sentence.

"I'm so sorry," the woman said. "How terrible for you. By the way, my name is Katerina."

"Hello, Katerina. That's a beautiful name." I told her mine. She smiled. "My name, Falk, is not beautiful. It sounds like *fuck*."

"So, you have money to stay in a hotel tonight?"

"Yes," I said. "Money. Lots of it. And tomorrow after the reading I will have more. Yes, lots and lots."

"The reading?"

I told her. And where.

"I've gone to lectures there. This is a very important place in Berlin."

"Yes," I said, muttering into my arm. "I am an important person who lectures in important places."

"You are an author?"

"Yes. I am an author. An important author. An important novelist. An important memoirist. An important adulterer? Yes, I tell you: I am important."

Again, the same tiresome emotional contractions in my chest, neck, face, as though a great hand of grief squeezed and squeezed like some invasive alien life-form rooting in me, producing from my strangled throat the same threatened Niagara of tears, the same torture chamber of shocked moans, and in my head images of Lena strapped into the airplane seat on the flight from Vienna, stepping into the chauffeured festival car in Innsbruck, sliding in next to me, my thigh touching hers, pressing up against her warmth, her long legs in a short skirt, high heels. I smiled and she hadn't moved away. That first time I saw her on the festival stage reading, clearly uncomfortable with public performance, out of her depth, a strange imaginative little girl in a beautiful woman's form. Later in Berlin, that one time between rapes, lying unclothed in my arms, soft eyes of gentle trust studying me, and her long hair fanned over the pillow, I loved her. Then, at the kitchen table her small hand touching fingertips to mine over cups of tea fed my sense that at last I had found someone with whom I could dwell love-paired in a solitary nest, drink tea, write books, fuck, two best-friend-lovers bound by a common empathy, accepting only the rare occasional visit from others, cultivating our own elfin world of two, making art, watching favorite films, arm in arm taking long walks along the boulevards of the major art capitals— New York, London, Paris, or in the South of France, some place where gardens fill all day with children, seniors, couples, dreamers, where in late spring strollers at dusk seem indistinguishable from the blooming flowers all around; where the moon skims over a lake like a small craft bearing lovers in restful embrace. Someplace where she loves me, the sound of my voice, the sight of my face, as much as I love her. These images and thoughts played in my brain like an old used LP of golden oldies, classic rock fished out of a thrift shop bin and spun at home for a lark on a refurbished outmoded turntable to a room full of snickering Manhattan trust fund hipsters. When I shared these hopes with Lena she had called them Disney-like middlebrow bourgeoise shit. They made her want to puke, she said.

I wept on, and the kind stranger, Katerina, let me, hand resting lightly on my arm, my grief borne on a floating sense of cosmic hopelessness, a dreadful pang of guilty shame, to be publicly falling apart in a seat of contemporary European enlightenment and economic power; where just generations ago goose-stepping National Socialists heartily abetted by the German people, die Volk, rapturously orchestrated the extermination of my people.

"I am so tired," I said. "So very, very tired. I want to go home. But where is that? I thought that she would be my home. What a thought!" Lifting my face, I grinned evilly at my own stupidity.

"I don't know what to say," said Katerina.

"No," I said. "No one does. Not even God."

"Why don't you call her?"

"Because I'm afraid to speak to her. I fear what she'll tell me. She says terrible things to me. She is very blunt."

"What's the worst that she can say?"

I told her what Lena had said, that she'll be in Cuba thinking of me while fucking Rolf.

Katerina's face blanched. "Don't call her," she blurted out. She looked down at her lap, then up. "I don't know what I'd do if someone I love told me that."

"I wanted to die. I still do, ever since she said it. I just can't seem to find the courage to finish the job."

Her hand on my arm squeezed firmly, as if to restrain me, hold me here to earth. "You mustn't say that. She is only one person. You are still a young man, I think. You mustn't die because of this."

I closed my eyes. "Katerina. Will you do me a favor?"

"Yes, of course. If I can."

"Do you have a sofa? I'll pay. Please, I don't really know anyone in Berlin. I don't want to be alone."

She thought. Decided. "There's no need to pay."

"All right."

Chapter 21

Her place was a small flat in Prenzlauer Berg, up three narrow flights of crumbling steps. She made up the couch for me, then went into the bathroom to change into her night clothes and emerged wearing over a flannel nightgown a jet-black kimono bursting with bright red and blue flowers. With her hair tied back, her face looked fresh, almost pretty. We sat at her kitchen table, quietly sipping chamomile tea and making light conversation. Then she said, "I hope you have a nice restful sleep. You will feel much better in the morning. Goodnight. Or, good afternoon. Sleep will do us both good. I'm also very tired."

At the thought of sleeping alone in the company of my crazy mind, I panicked and said, "It's only 1:30 in the afternoon. Do you always go to sleep this early?"

"No. But I'm very tired. When I wake up, I'll make us some food. Okay?"

"Yes."

I lay there in the dark for some time. Then I said, "Katerina?"

"Yes?"

"You're up?"

"Yes."

"Can I come there with you? I don't want to be alone."

After a long struggling pause, she said, "You have no diseases?"

"None I know of."

"Okay."

This time my member performed as it should. I felt large and dominant as I drove myself home in her. But as the song goes, "It's not the meat, it's the motion." I had lost my erotic rhythmic sense and, when I came in her with a loud cry, she was silent. Selfishly, I rolled off her with a slight sense of remorse but didn't really care.

She didn't seem to mind, was content as we lay in each other's arms with a warm glow on our skins, at peace. At least the agonies with Lena could not taunt me. She whom I was born to love seemed far from me now, thanks to destiny's false turn, a bad joke with no punchline. In fact, Lena was nothing like what I thought a love should be; but this stranger, Katerina, by a simple act of compassionate faith proved that the love I had sought for all my life can and does exist, at least in some form. Or perhaps, on her part, it was recklessness, or naïveté, or simple lonely desperation. She was, after all, not nearly as attractive as Lena. At the thought of this, I began to sicken just a tad. Also, something seemed off in Katerina's odor, I noted; her skin exuded a distinct hint of acridness and the more I inhaled it the stronger it seemed. An ammonia reek. I grew nauseated, not from the stench so much as the thought of spending the rest of my life with that odor in my nose. But why think of that? A least for now, it was tolerable, even an improvement. Anything was better than Lena.

Still, the acrid smell troubled me. I slept that night with my back turned to her.

The next day, I gave my reading in the prestigious Literarische Colloquium to which Katerina came proudly on my arm. Attractively dressed in matching black turtleneck dress and high heels, she sat in the front row. She had terrific legs which I ogled as I read, and occasionally I smiled at her, though not as proudly or possessively as I would have had her face been a little prettier. She smiled back. Guilt soured my smile a bit though, for I knew that I could not spend my life with the acrid smell she gave off in bed and that I now smelled too, just faintly, despite her perfume. She was no kid, was in her mid-thirties probably. I guessed that the odor problem wasn't new but chronic and so incurable. Also, probably, she'd want kids. Perhaps they too would smell. Our little loving life would soon become a hell of baby clothes and crib, with a smelly little beast in there jumping up and down, shrieking and laughing and crapping all over himself. With my luck, I'd probably slip on an alphabet block, end up in a wheelchair for life. I knew: my gift for falling was irrevocable. The dice had been cast, the fates played knucklebones with my destiny, rattling my days in their cup, my hopes tossed up against a wall, coming up craps. From here on, every step I took could end in the abyss. I was no longer safe, between jihadists and advancing age, one or another, or some accident, could take my life.

In the back row I spotted Lena, seated with Rolf, but pretended not to see her and struggled fiercely to keep my eyes on Katerina throughout the reading. I told myself that I was over that now, over her; that Katerina's presence bolstered my resolve, made me brave. But during my onstage interview and the audience Q&A, I kept glancing grimly at Lena and with outright hatred at Rolf. When I ogled Katerina's stunning legs, I glanced furtively at Lena to see if she'd noticed, hoping to make her jealous. But she looked completely unmoved.

Of course, Katerina took any sign of attention from me as proof of love which, in fact, I didn't feel. I hoped only to make Lena suffer. On the other hand, knowing Lena, probably she'd already decided that Katerina's unremarkable looks were no competition and had determined to challenge her in open combat for my soul. Of course, she knew she'd already won, despite that after the event, before adjourning to a signing table in the lobby stacked high with my books, I made an elaborate display of holding Katerina close and planting a long drop-dead kiss on her peach-fuzzed mouth. For the briefest instant my eyes scanned the back row for Lena, but she and the poststructuralist six-pack tennis prick were gone.

After the event Katerina and I joined the mandatory dinner out with the colloquium staff. Everyone seemed to like her and she, I could tell, thoroughly enjoyed herself. But all I could think of was her acrid smell, her not-so-pretty face, the fuzz, how poorly she stacked up against Lena, who smelled delicious and in a short dress and heels looked wonderful. Nonetheless, I gave myself to the occasion with its fine food, repartee with famous Berlin authors in attendance, and tried to enjoy that all-too-rare sense of doing work important to Literature, though I knew, in fact, that neither my readings nor books nor anything that anyone ever wrote would ever change the world a single jot. The pen is less mighty than Life; has in fact become obsolete. Cursive writing is no longer even taught in school. And certainly, the keyboard is not mightier than the M16. The Internet has destroyed whatever power authors once had. Besides, how many authors at their desks, believing their pens mighty, held it up to guard their face when armed thugs appeared to beat them senseless and sent their pen clattering impotently across the floor? No pen ever stopped a bullet or was of much use when the State's torturer applied the cattle prod. Yes, an author's words may reach a stranger's eyes long after the fact of his death, but no one hears his agonized screams en route to the torture chamber.

That night at Katerina's, in a desolate mood of devouring libidinous rage I dragged her brutally to the bed, tore off her panties in my fist, hoisted her black high heels over my shoulders and thrust myself hungrily into her. She seemed to enjoy it, and afterward she passed out, slept with an angelic look, but still exuded that mineral smell.

It was quite unpleasant.

Chapter 22

Quietly, I slipped from bed, dressed, and left. Katerina, who had imbibed a bit too much the night before, slept soundly, never seemed to notice my exit. Or, just as likely, she did but pretended sleep in order to avoid a humiliating encounter; knew that I had no intention of returning.

At Lena's, I rang the intercom, was buzzed in. On the third floor, I knocked at her immense door. It opened.

There stood Hubert.

"You," he said, voice quavering.

In an instant I understood he knew everything.

"Me," I said.

"She's not here."

"Do you know when she'll return?"

"Probably not tonight. She hasn't been home since she went to your reading last night." His eyes clouded.

I nodded with sympathy. I had liked Hubert the first time we met, and now, the second time, liked him again. We were both victims of a witch's spell. "She wasn't with me," is all I said.

"Well, come in," he said wearily. "Just come in." I knew that weariness, knew it well.

"Are you sure?"

"Come in."

We sat in the kitchen where the last time I was here she served me tea and fed me after our weird attempts to make love.

He poured hot tea from a kettle for the two of us. And Lena was in everything: the rough wooden table, the cups, an old printing press storage chest with draws labeled with her handwriting: "coffee," "tea," "herbs," and so forth. On the walls hung strange public health posters from her beloved India. I thought of her fellating Rolf in a New Delhi slum. Surrounded on all sides, we circled our wagons.

"She's with him," he said.

"So, you know about him? I thought you didn't." I think neither of us could bear to utter his name aloud.

He nodded. "I've always known about him. It's been five years. But you were a surprise."

"I'm sorry," I said. "I love her, Hubert. And I've never felt so utterly miserable."

"You don't look very well."

I looked up at him, tears filling my eyes. "Why should you care how I look or how I feel? How can you think about anyone but yourself in this kind of situation?"

"Actually, the only relief is not to think of myself but of someone else. Yes, even you. So, you came because you love her and thought that since the marriage is dead it would be okay to take her from me."

"Yes."

"And then you found out about him."

"Yes."

"And that changed everything."

"Yes."

He smiled. "You are a very moralistic adulterer."

We both sat in silence after that, sipping tea. There was nothing more to say. He was a better man than I. When I rose to leave, he accompanied me to the door, held it open for my departure.

"She loves you," he said. "She loves me too. And she loves Rolf."

"You have met him?"

"I first saw him at one of her readings. I knew right away. Of course, she denied it. That is who she is. And none of it is really love. None of it. She loves no one but herself. That is Lena. A sociopath. She has this thing about money. Who doesn't? But to the point of mental illness, and she thinks her legs are too short. If I had to sum her up, I'd say, "An unscrupulous Scrooge obsessed with the length of her legs." You're very tall. Probably, that's what she likes. There is no way you could know. About Rolf, personally, I dislike him, and I sense that you would too if you had the chance to speak with him, as I did. Yes, don't look so shocked. She brought him here once, just the way she brought you. She insisted that he stay, said that he was a famous philosopher. She slipped into his room at night while I pretended sleep. They didn't even hide the noises. They took to each other in this lizard-like, cold-blooded way. They were made for each other. There may even be others. I'll never know exactly who or how many."

"Tell me," I said, half smiling. "Do you think her legs are too short?"

"Yes. You?"

"No. I think they're perfect."

He grinned sadly. "The mystery of personal preference."

We both stood there, our hearts sundered. I said, "I don't understand. Do you?"

"Never," he said. "Never will I understand. Never. And least of all why I am still so in love with her."

"Yes," I said. "Never."

Chapter 23

When He created the heavens and the earth, God must have
been a nervous wreck who'd fallen off his meds. He made
us with a cosmic pointless whimpering in the bloodstream of lust-
tormented flesh, minus all trace of holiness, sanctity, or goodness.
Nor is the sun a cheerful comfort zone but a heartbroken inferno
convulsing in the black refrigeration of Space, fending off contractions of ceaseless anguished hope sent up as desperate prayers
from the beaks of hapless orphaned life-forms ambulating in a
void. Funny that microbes of bikini-clad humans pleasurably bask
in the weakened filtered beams of this suffering fiery sun and
imagine it moral, decent, loving, good, even something to worship, make sacrifice to, sometimes even their own children. And
so, too, when I rise, I come not like a flower (although a flower is
its own defense of violent color, its petals rotor blades of potential
insect decapitation) but like a black minotaur of charging lethal-
ity, my mind a waving gun, and memories that I choose to forget
mentally arranged for execution, a quick dispatching shot to the
neck, while on a Mediterranean cave wall hidden from the searing
sky, rabbis in long black frock coats intone the Hebraic sonatas of
messianic hope that at any instant now, or ten thousand eons
hence, the murderous scorpions of the world will transform into
one immense and joyous butterfly.

But until then, each one a sainted martyr, the rabbis fall, stung
with erotic poisons whose effects torment them well beyond what
any living being should have to endure. From such fallen and
afflicted Kabbalists am I spiritually descended, a vessel of
unhinged agonizing contradictions, so that I know that what I call
"God" proceeds from out of the demonic cosmology of my unex-
pressed, unexamined, unprosecuted or proclaimed astral pie chart
of fickle and unknowable destiny, neither good, bad, moral, nor

immoral but a heedless celestial drama composed of scenes to be played out before no one, for no one's delectation, in the empty theater of the night.

In other words, some bioengineering Guissepo constructed my psyche like a hapless marionette doomed time and again to relive the same nose-distending lie ad nauseum, suffer the consequences of my long-discredited, even denigrated, most cherished notion that love, true love—love that desires and pursues what it seeks— can ever exist or be mine. Time and again must love be proved, through the shattering of my heart and nerves, to be a celluloid Hollywood pipe dream, like the ending of the film *Breakfast at Tiffany's*, where George Peppard, Audrey Hepburn, and the no-name cat all squeeze together for a long true kiss in the rain as "Moon River" croons and its arpeggios induce in me a tearful psychotic rhapsody that is itself a black deception, for the only true angels I know of are not Moon River Huckleberry friends but train station whores who weep privately, inconsolably, hunched and alone, in a corner of the night, broken forever by unrelenting need and unfulfillable hope, each whore a dead planet yearning for a river of her own to drown in.

Her name is Lena. A furtive hunger. My utterly alien needs threaten the pattern of her interstellar constellation in which I, Hubert, and Rolf revolve around her cold dead star.

I want trust, loyalty, exclusivity, all that Lena rejects. In fact, at times when my own mounting selfish desire becomes suicidal ideation Lena's need grows elliptical; threatens to tear free of her orbit, and shatter everything, everyone, including herself.

So, I weep alone. The strange thing is, sadly, that we humans are, after all, just habitual little beasts grown accustomed to certain comforts that we return to again and again, doomed to revisit our ghosts in the motions of certain rituals of relived emotions long past any usefulness. We do so numbly and grievously because once we have loved we do not stop loving. Lucky are those rare few who find love early on, never need another. I wanted that. We all do. All our failed loves reside within us, sitting shivah in an emotional purgatory.

I never returned to Katerina, but left Berlin and wandered as before, from reading to book signing, interview to festival. Regardless of where I went, no matter where I happened to be, at 3 or 4 a.m., I rose, as before, went to my laptop, and up came the Skype page on which we had digitally inscribed our fluctuating affair, in long chat strings of intense desire, a call and response of impossible feelings.

I sat in some hotel room staring at the ghosted picture of her Skype profile headshot encircled and slashed by a single diagonal black stripe to indicate that I had blocked her, and yet irrationally I hoped I don't know what to find there. I rummaged through my email box—she was blocked there too. And the same for Facebook. And then I scrounged the Internet for any news of her, any reference to some interview with her or book announcement or event in which she might appear. Nothing. It was as though she had ceased to exist. Her whole life had ground to a halt. And I guessed that probably she was with Rolf in Central America by now, third-world-fucking her way through impoverished wastelands populated by lepers, drug gangs, and winged monkeys swooping down to her from the darkening sky. Or was she now back in Berlin, at home cozy-coupling with poor miserable Hubert, who, knowing all, was shivering with phantasmagoric plots, demanding justice, accusing himself of failure, and blaming the economy, the politics of the day, religion, art, nationalism, modernism, Angela Merkel, Walter Benjamin, or God knows what else for his catastrophic matrimonial attachment to her.

As I wander from city to city, awake late at night in hotel rooms, event invitations continue pouring in despite poor Schroeder's efforts to save me from myself. And somehow, improbably, my book's reception improves, its reputation grows. By now the German translation of *Kike* has developed something of a cult following. Sales are brisk. Schroeder is ecstatic. We Skype.

"I feel like I am gaining a bestseller but losing an author. Your book has become a minor hit. I'll send you the latest reviews. All at once the major newspapers in Germany and Austria ran big front-page reviews. They're calling it a 'Post-Holocaust classic.'

Praise is pouring in. I'll forward it to you. But you yourself look like shit, if you must know."

"Thanks. I've been recognized and stopped for autographs once or twice in the street. One requested me to write on the back of a billing envelope: 'To Emilia, kisses from your favorite Kike!' Post-Holocaust my ass. There is no such thing. The mass graves are still out there, the pulverized bones of the murdered at the bottom of rivers, ponds, and lakes. And in your country and in Germany, in their nice flats, the retired killers live on their considerable pensions from IG Farben, too old to wipe themselves, getting wrapped in adult diapers by loving Czech caretakers who now and then give them a nice little hand jerk and happy ending spritz just to relieve the pressure on their withered nut sacks."

"What are you talking about? I thought you didn't drink."

"Don't worry. I'm still sober."

"Well, what is that behind you? That weird round light?"

"It's a weird round light."

"It looks like something from outer space and your face looks like Peter Lorre in Fritz Lang's *M*. Look, let me go back to choosing your hotels. I'll book you. Obviously, the firm will pay now that you're making us a little money. The tour isn't done, even if it should be, because frankly I don't think you'll survive. You're a weak man. You let that cunt destroy you. But you must go on. By the way, Gerhardt contacted me. Give him a ring up. He wants to invite you to something."

"What?"

"Call him. He's your friend, no?"

Berlin-Graz-Berlin

Chapter 24

I called Gerhardt. We were invited to Graz, to the university, to do two consecutive nights onstage and were requested to be there on Wednesday. It was Monday. Again, no time for publicity. I expected an audience of three persons, if that.

In Graz, Gerhardt and I met at the Hotel Wiesses, our favorite place in that town. The university had booked us into the most expensive suites available. They were like huge apartments, really. We were received as visiting royalty.

The first night's event before a full house was broadcast live throughout Austria. Suddenly, I was something of a celebrity, for a few weeks anyway.

The next morning, we met for breakfast in the hotel's excellent dining room. But Gerhardt was not his usual spry self; he looked downcast, withdrawn. I had noticed it last night too. We shook hands, sat, each with a plate heaped with breakfast food from the first-class smorgasbord.

"That was some night, huh?" he said.

"Some night. But what happened to you? I'm jealous. It must be a woman. I thought I was the only one who's supposed to look like shit."

He nodded, no offense taken. "You still don't look too well yourself."

"I'm not. I've only just now gotten used to the suffering. But what's troubling you? It's a woman, right?"

He grimaced painfully. "I'm to receive an honorary doctorate from the university."

The news brought me upright. "How extraordinary! Gerhardt, congratulations!"

He waved this off with a shy gesture. "No, no, no. It's ridiculous. If it didn't come with a lecture for which I'll be paid a lot I would never have agreed to such bullshit."

"Still, it's no small thing."

He looked at me. "That's not all. I met someone. It's ridiculous."

"But you have Elke already. She's a knockout. Why would you need someone else?"

He shook his head in bewilderment. "I don't. But I can't help myself. It's crazy. I met her at a writer's conference in Paris. She's Hungarian. The entire conference we only spoke once. I gave her my phone number to have further conversation or to meet. But she never called. When I did, she didn't answer. Then, an hour after the conference, she texts to say that she misses me like crazy, must see me. We begin to text day and night. The texting becomes more and more intense. It becomes like fucking. We are fucking each other with texts. The next thing I know I'm on a plane to Budapest. We meet in a hotel. She has a boyfriend. She doesn't want to fuck. We lie in bed together all night, talking, holding each other. She pushes away my hands. Finally, she gives me a blow job. Why don't we consummate our love, I ask her, in the traditional manner?"

"You mean fuck."

"Yes. Exactly."

"And . . ."

"She can't," she says. "That is for the boyfriend. She is a loyal person."

"But the blow job," I say.

"That is not disloyal, she claims. That is just like a kiss, no more. An innocent indiscretion."

Sadly, I shook my head. "These women that you and I attract, what planet are they from?"

Gerhardt shrugged. "Now I can't stop thinking about her."

"They say that blow jobs are more addictive than fucking. Smart girl."

"I'm hooked," he said. "I'm going through withdrawal, like a junky."

"You're the William Burroughs of head."

"And you. You have heard from you know who? Dare I say her name?"

"No to both questions."

"I don't know whether to say sorry or congratulations."

"Both, I think."

"Yes, undoubtably. My impression is that she is not ever going to leave her husband or lover. Why would she? She's had one for decades and the other for years. She's known you but a few short months and of those, really, just a few days face to face and all the rest of the time on Skype. What I don't understand—and if you don't wish to answer then don't: Why did you not visit her again in Berlin? Surely there must have been a window in your schedule . . . ?"

So, I told him what until then no one knew of my humiliating attempt to purchase a gun and then to see her and how it ended, the homeless night on Berlin streets, and come morning, plucked from oblivion by Katerina, a perfect stranger, a wallflower whom I ruthlessly, unceremoniously dumped.

He looked down sadly at his food. "That is terrible. And what you did to this poor Katerina." He lifted a piece of sausage to his mouth, chewed thoughtfully, and said. "You are surely going to hell, you know this, yes?"

My face fell into my hands. I sat so, a man with hands praying to his own face. I heard Gerhardt set down his fork. Through my fingers I spied a passing university student waitress, formally dressed in a white blouse, black skirt, black shoes, pretending not to see my stricken posture as she refilled our coffee cups. I lifted my face, which must have looked awful, dropped my hands, and stared directly at her with tears. Briskly, she looked away.

I turned my red wolf eyes on Gerhardt who could barely bring himself to look into them. "I must go see her again. But if I do, I feel quite sure I will not survive the experience."

"Then don't be a fool. Don't do it. You're too important to waste yourself on such a vicious little tart. To hell with her!"

"But you don't understand."

"But I do."

I knew that he understood, had no doubt felt the same in the past, time and again. He stood, came around to my side of the table, gently placed hands on my shoulders. "Let's go for a walk." Urging me to my feet, he led me out of the dining room and then from the hotel.

Chapter 25

We went along quaint old streets of the university town. Students everywhere lounged in the South Austrian sunshine or rushed about on errands of monumental academic significance to them but which meant nothing to the world, to life, and of course that's the appeal of the academic way. It made me nostalgic for the ivory tower where you could spend years happily divorced from Reality, squandering as much time as you please on reading, drinking, fornication, and sleeping. During my own school years after the army I always had a campus girlfriend who was really just a sex partner; I did little socializing, wrote constantly, and the successes, albeit modest ones, came; but soon I was lifted from out of the innocent concerns of a student writer into the thankless and pressurized life of a professional author who is only as good as his next book. Most of my time was spent in some flat somewhere, whether in Jerusalem or Paris or San Francisco, which became my favorite place to write in complete isolation, without even the company of fellow writers who, try as they did to fraternize with me, I could ignore like so many apparitional distracting wastes of time, having little use for their opinions, which I found worthless; I almost never attended their readings, which gained me a reputation for arrogant aloofness. In truth, only an appearance before an audience on stage could dispel my crippling chronic loneliness. I began to pursue appearances on the reading circuit, became known as one who was very good at it, and while I did fine in Israel and all right financially in America, once my books began to appear in Europe, there I made the real killing—Europe was ripe for me—and I could tour, like now, almost at will and for longer and longer periods of time, sometimes up to half a year. Finally, it got to where, if I had wanted, I could have remained in Europe working indefinitely. I had only to fly out every few months, stay in San Francisco or Tel Aviv for a few days, and return, just to satisfy EU immigration controls.

But though it was now lovely to walk the streets talking about our respective broken hearts—for Gerhardt opened up about the ruinous impact of the Hungarian upon his own fragile nerves— our conversation underscored for me that, really, on this earth there is nothing more contemptable than two writers bloviating to each other about their romantic failures unless they are both onstage getting paid for it. After all, we are inherently selfish. Brutally so. I've never truly gone public in any kind of graphic detail but then I'd never had occasion to until now. No one had ever affected me as deeply or destructively as Lena.

We stopped beside a bench, sat, and Gerhardt looked down reflectively at the pressed palms of his hands. "Have you ever seriously considered suicide?"

"Often."

He nodded. "Did you ever come close?"

"Yes, once. I owned a five-shot .38 British Webley. A real antique but it worked just fine. One night, after a breakup with a woman in Jerusalem whom I didn't even particularly care for, while listening to Vivaldi's *Four Seasons*, I removed the pistol, ejected four rounds, spun the chamber, put the barrel to my head and fired. And then twice more. For a few hours my exhilaration at beating Death was great. Then boredom returned. Emptiness."

"That sounds like depression."

"No. It was awareness."

"Of what?"

"That we are incapable of providing each other with the love we desperately need. And what's worse, that even if we could it would not matter. We would allow some mere hint of tenderness from a stranger to tear us from ourselves, out of our very life, and lead us on a futile trek through hell for more empty calories, much as you're doing now with your profitless Hungarian."

Gerhardt said nothing for a time, his downturned face reflective. Then, "But why?"

"Why the need? Or why the inability to meet it in each other?

Or why the addiction to suffering? Or why, if we had love, still we'd throw it all away for an illusion? Our mothers," I said. "And because we are inherently flawed, fallible. Animals are not. Animals are perfectly what they are. But not humans. We think and feel, speculate, and evaluate and forecast, damned by desire and imagination. Sometimes we believe that we ourselves are what made this universe, rather than understand that we were only born into it for a brief while. What then made all of this? Something did. It didn't simply spring from a void. Nothingness cannot generate anything other than itself. Call it, then, what you will, but I call it God. Call it by any name except your own or for that matter another human being's because then you are laying ground for a Hitler, Stalin, or Trump. But call it by some mumbo jumbo name and pray to it and spend some portion of each day contemplating it, trying to understand what sort of universal principles God hopes would rule human undertakings. Love. Justice. Faith. Self-discipline. Tolerance. That, perhaps, most of all. And how one might demonstrate these in our own affairs. Why should we do this? Because without some sort of higher code by which to live we are at the mercy of lizard brain, of fight or flight, of greed, of weird urges that should never see the light but which without the firm hand of God and principle will wreak havoc upon everyone, everything, each other, worst of all, perhaps, on ourselves."

"Religion. That is your solution?" Gerhardt looked disappointed, even offended. His eyes grew moist. "Sometimes I think there's no point in living."

"I think you're right! That's why some sort of universal principles to follow out of hell are so necessary."

Gerhardt looked at me, his eyes childlike, vulnerable. "But you are the most unprincipled person I have ever met."

I nodded bitterly, told him that he was right. But that didn't mean, I said, that I couldn't recognize his condition, which I knew well, or the probable solution to it. The same sort of crushed child as dwelled in him occupied me. Not, as the Buddhists disdainfully call it, a "Hungry Ghost" but a Deprived Innocent, needing love in a depraved world yet incapable of giving it, uncertain how to get it. And running around scared, occasionally panicking. Of course, the world condemns the innocent as culprits, declares us depraved for needing love, for grieving that we cannot seem to find it anywhere; tells us that it is better to give than to receive, better to love than to be loved. In other words, if you expect to get love, FORGET IT! Everyone exhorts us instead to burrow yet deeper into our depleted human reserves to dredge up the last of our humanity and scatter it to the desert, the sand, the vast desolation of human affairs, for the hyenas and vultures to lap up. Until there is nothing left of us but the grinning and fossilized Jolly Roger skull, stripped of all emotion, all need, all hope, all illusion—an ornament to adorn the hellish gates of the portal to nirvana. Such a smile knows the pitiless world. Such a smile warns, "Abandon all hope." Such a smile tells you no one can be counted upon. Love is unavailable, period. Happy are those who permit this truth to penetrate their thick skulls and act accordingly. Fuck for pleasure, not affection. Seduce to use, not possess. Lucky are those who, rather than require fidelity from a partner, couldn't care less and fuck whomever they want, when they like, and lie about it. It is the knowledge of all this and nothing else that drives those of us with fragile, too-romantic nerves to the very brink, where suicide seems not so much a tragic outcome as a long overdue relief and blessing. For who among us is born indifferent to devotion, loyalty, fidelity, love, closeness, togetherness, monogamy, and pops out of the womb genetically engineered to chop through the opposite sex, wielding his or her sexual organ like a machete, is a pathological narcissist, a chronic cheat, a psychopathic sexually sadistic serial killer, a habitual rapist. The rest of us like wide-eyed simpletons waddle around with outstretched arms, expecting a loving universe to gather us up and cuddle our cute and trusting selves. But the only response it offers back is a swift kick to the teeth, a nightstick in the groin.

Gerhard nodded, shaken, his eyes moist. "You are right. This is also my experience. I could not have put it in so many words, but I too have never really known true love from a single woman. Each one offered at the beginning what seemed like love. But soon we both knew that it wasn't real at all. Just a fantasy powered by greed, need, and vanity. Neither of us, truly, was capable of it. And I followed along, down the path of destruction. Again, and again. Knowing it was futile. But unable to stop."

"Yes," I said. "Followed down the nervy path of self-destruction into cataclysms of emotional rollercoasting trauma and never once did one of those women put on the brakes. Each rode the lethal wave to the annihilating end. And like me you watched them do it. You were completely helpless not to. We played out our parts in our own destruction, you and me. But they—they tried to reduce us to nothing. They tried to grind us down to an agonized heap of rags and bones. And we let them. I let them. You let them. I never felt I had a choice. At that point when I had chosen death over life, I encouraged them to obliterate me. Why not? It is the nihilist's final dream of joy. Every last vestige of self-respect went out the window. Every terrible thing that could be said or done, was. My humiliation was complete. When I was with them, I feared abandonment and when they were not present the abandonment was unbearable. Any assertion of their self or personal will stabbed me like a knife. If they were present, I feared their leaving. If they returned, I feared their staying. My only freedom was to destroy the relationship by spurring them to be rid of me. The only cure for my dread of abandonment was to be abandoned. Then, I could reinvent myself, even just briefly. I could taste an illusory freedom, spend time with myself in narcissism, onanism, but inevitably the horrors of loneliness returned and brought, once more, the terrors of love."

Gerhardt, speechless, was so dejected by the time we reached our hotel that he excused himself and retired to his room until the second night's event, at which, because we are pros, we both performed spectacularly, two jolly fun-loving strutting nihilistic existentialists but now and then our eyes locked in despair at the horrible state of our personal affairs, the failures awaiting us in our respective love lives. It is no easy thing to see the last vestige of a defeated romantic hope crushed dead by a tyrannical black boot of undeniable reality.

Berlin

Chapter 26

From city to city I went, avoiding Skype, keeping her account blocked, though I hadn't deleted it. Why, why, why had I not deleted it?

One night I unblocked it and SMS pleas for me to call her erupted and metastasized in little blue balloons all over my screen. The luminous green dot indicating that she was available appeared beneath her photograph, which she had changed. In the new picture she looked haunted, wounded, tragically beautiful.

I paused to reflect but was unable to think clearly. Jittery, I sat staring at her Skype page, at the fossil strings of our endless dialogues. Should I hit the call button now, ring her up? A hundred voices shouted in my head that she would not simply answer but would run to respond. For one moment I relished my power to level her if I wished to—at least to as low as she had brought me; lower perhaps. I wanted to see her weep just one more time and after that to see her crawl. But what sort of power is it to be isolated in one's lovelessness and injury, having recourse to inflict pain on she whom one most wants to love? I knew that even if I had her stretched on a rack, howling for mercy, inside I would feel nothing and would only love her. What then would be the point of contacting her? Revenge struck me as the very essence of impotence, not power. For all I wanted was genuine care, not hate. But should I ring her anyway? Now? Ever? Why? I tried to recall the horrific agonies that I had endured at her hands but for some reason could recollect only vaguely some of the pain that she had inflicted. I mainly remembered the love.

I saw sharply in my mind her slender body, small firm breasts, large round nipples; saw the delicate "V" that I was now desperate to enter for a silken ride, and to penetrate and stab with murderously possessive pelvic thrusts to the very core of her, but even as I considered the possible adverse consequences of letting her back into my life, I dismissed them as irrelevant, as though my pain did not count, and in rapid blurry snippets of rushing mental footage saw snatches of her Hubert's numbed face, then gross images of Rolf's taut white buttocks clenched as he rose and drove into her with his horse cock and saw her hands grip his back as I had hoped that she would grip mine, and saw her face as she smiled at me and said, "I will think of you as I fuck him," and felt tears well up in my chest and eyes and then the dim phantom of an unquenchable, almost homicidal fury—for really I had never once imagined hate as my default emotion but it seemed to be the sum total of all emotions now. It arose in me and though I now grasped that it was not for love but only for hate, I pushed that call button. With a feeling of incredulous outrage, perhaps more at myself than at her, I heard the Skype ring moaning through the Internet, then saw the familiar whirling white dots circling the screen's black center and in the upper left corner a timer began to keep digital track and as if from thin air I saw her face materialize, so grateful to see me, and smiling more prettily than I'd ever seen her before.

At first I stared coldly, then with a smile, and she smiled back and nodded, as before, as if to signal some unspoken understanding and as always I wondered what exactly that understanding was, for I had never really had any idea and when I had asked she had refused to answer, as if offended by the question, as if I should know better. Was it, "Yes, our souls understand everything? Yes, we love each other and only we can know what that means?" But my soul didn't know. Now, I smiled from nervousness I think, not camaraderie or love. From panic. The smile of prey faced by its stalker whom it hoped, believed, it had eluded only to meet its great ravenous countenance peering from the bush; an unnerved smile before an impending and cruel death; a last instant of jokey refusal to countenance the agonizing ordeal about to ensue.

"So?" I said to break the silence.

She hesitated. Then said, "I'm okay. My editor likes my new

manuscript. We met on Thursday. She wants a few changes. I'm trying to make them now."

"Are they good changes? Improvements? Do you agree with them?"

"I do, I think."

"You don't know?"

"No." Then, "Why are you calling me?"

"I don't know."

"We make each other very unhappy."

"Yes."

Then, as though arguing with some impartial and observing referee in the room, she said, "We're Jews. It's what we do."

"Do you really believe that?" I asked.

"Yes."

But though I didn't agree I did not push further—as always accepted from her the unacceptable, even tried to make it my truth. Okay, all right, our unhappiness is directly attributable to the fact that she and I are Jews and unhappiness in love, in all things, is what we Jews specialize in. A part of me whispered in protest of this atrocious nonsense. But I went forward with her vision anyway, adopted it, because it was dark and sinking. I felt captivated, fascinated, by her infiltrating poison, permeating the entire fabric of my being with unmentionable urges, memories not mine, sickened dreams, a creeping coughing psychological and spiritual possession of my cells, my very DNA.

"I'm afraid to say what is on my mind, the question haunting me . . ."

Her face paled. "What is it?"

"Your plan . . ."

"What plan?"

"You were going to fly to Panama with Rolf."

"Why do you have to go back to that old history?"

"You were going to go to Panama with Rolf for three months, then return to Berlin, then go to New York to meet me and live with me there for five months and the entire time you planned to keep Hubert in the dark, cheat on him with two men, and live off his money. How do you do that? I mean, ethically, psychologically, how . . . if I could understand that . . . but I can't . . ."

"You didn't call because you miss me. You called to interrogate me. Like a courtroom. I feel your hatred."

"If you could just explain to me . . ."

"You don't understand me. You never will. We are not the same. I was wrong about you."

I stared at something off screen: the neutral gray wall of my hotel room.

She asked, "Where are you?"

I didn't reply.

"What are you thinking? You look so sad. Stop making yourself sick with sad thoughts."

I looked back at the screen, at her. "Do you know why you and I so often feel poorly in these conversations?"

"You are the one who cries all the time."

"You've done your share."

"Only with you. I never cried before. Never!"

"Because we each need from the other what the other can never give."

"And what do I need that you cannot give?"

"Trust."

"I don't need trust. What do you need from me that I cannot give?"

"Trustworthiness."

"I have never lied to you!"

"Perhaps. But each day, each hour and minute that you lie to yourself you are lying to me too. I can't do this anymore. I must leave. I don't want to be destroyed. I don't know why I called. Now I do. To tell you that I don't want to be destroyed. I won't let you destroy me with your lies and disloyalty. I know now that I called to say to you for once and all good-bye. I'm finished. We're through."

Her face convulsed. She fell from her chair to her knees and clasped her hands in a begging plea. "No, no, no, no, please, my

love, no, don't, don't break up with me, don't break up with me
. . ." and began to sob.

"I'm sorry," I said, upset by this image of her. I did not want to
see her like this. She must love me deeply to resort to such a
humiliating move, I told myself, to be so reduced, so without self-
respect. I thought that only I was capable of such self-humiliation.
"It must end. We repeat ourselves over and over and over. We
return to the same insanity again and again. It's useless to go on.
Don't try to contact me. You will never see me again."

She cried out, "Noooooooo . . . PLEASE!" as my screen clicked
dead. I shut off the laptop, silenced my cell phone. For a full ten
minutes I sat there shaken, horrified, unaware of being alive,
unsure if I even breathed, my mind a gray blank neural wall but
gloating a little to have inflicted such a decisive wound. Then,
from within my chest, stomach, and head a great rolling wave of
sorrow burst my dam, engulfed me, and I sat there quietly in pain
until not a single tear was left in me. I rose unsteadily to my feet,
looked at my phone. She had called ten times. Texted four. There
would be emails. I fell into my bed. On my cell phone I surfed
YouTube videos of masked ISIS executioners sawing off the heads
of Americans, Egyptians, Syrians, Australians, Libyans, Poles,
Brits, French, men, women, children, Japanese, Muslims, Chris-
tians, Jews, and secularists, and muttering aloud to myself wondered what happened, when did the world start to fall, for it is
falling, falling, and I fell off to sleep in darkness dreaming of terrible undreamed-of things, hoping never to wake again.

When I awoke it was quite late, heading into the morning
hours. For a moment I could not recall what city I was in or the
name of the hotel. And then, I remembered, though to know
didn't really seem much to matter.

Tel Aviv

Chapter 27

Adelphi, an oddly named Israeli, contacted me via social media messaging about another of my books, *The Boozer*, which she insisted had changed her life, a claim that I received with skepticism dashed with a pinch of vanity and not a little pride.

Immediately, I clicked onto her name which took me to her profile page. I checked her photo: hot blonde. Tattoos from shoulder to lower back. Her self-description read that she was a therapeutic hypnotist for a reputable Tel Aviv homeopathic clinic. She was twenty-eight years old—my junior by many years. I switched back to her message, reread it several times for tone, personality, social dynamic and concluded that she had positioned herself as a submissive "acolyte" inviting me to occupy a mentoring position for the sole purpose of seducing me into a sexual liaison and eventual long-term partnership.

I waited several days, to intensify her anticipation. When, at last, I did respond with a dinner invite she shot back a grateful gushing affirmative reply: "What a privilege, such a great honor. Thank you so much for getting back to me. I saw your recent interview online on the BBC website. It was amazing . . . yes, yes, yes to dinner." On the appointed night I arrived a few minutes late, so as not to appear as eager as I felt to penetrate her. Casually, I sidled up behind her. She stood in front of the Café Albert, on Rehov Einstein 40, looking anxiously about for my approach. When I tapped her on the shoulder she turned, surprised, and right off, I noted that she bore little resemblance to her Facebook selfie. Not that she was any less attractive, but in a different way, her hair blonder, her face and figure fuller, not as streamlined. Clearly, she had put on weight, was eating from frustration.

She said my name. I said hers. We stood observing each other, both pleased. She had fantastic green eyes. She smiled. I smiled. It happened that I had to do a reading that night at Tel Aviv University. Would she mind terribly escorting me to the event as my date, I asked. It would take about two hours, after which we could have dinner.

She beamed, for she knew by this sudden rushing invite that she was pleasing enough to me to be seen with her at a very public (and no doubt important) literary occasion.

We went, walking slowly, discovering each other's presence. Along the way I took her hand. We kissed. When we arrived shortly, she was hugging my arm; we seemed glamorous: the older writer with the hot young ingenue—but who, after all, was not so innocent—and we seemed to be a happy couple. I could tell: she very much wanted us to appear so to others, as well as to herself. The prospect of what awaited me later that night made me tumescent. Cameras of news photographers clicked.

Of course, I knew nothing whatever about this person. Nonetheless, during my reading I kept looking her way, which drew the eyes of the audience to her, and Adelphi basked in the attention, particularly that of several not-unattractive ladies who were clearly steamed to find me so completely absorbed and unavailable.

I screwed her in my hotel that night. I felt nothing for her, really, it was all in my head—the fantasy of old Picasso with the young wife, rejuvenated, exploding with creative fire. She seemed excited by my evident ardor which made it easy and enhanced her pleasure. I came on her stomach and wiped myself off on the starched hotel bedsheet. Then after a brief pause, we went a second round during which I felt the unpleasant wetness of my expelled cold cum from the first tumble. She moaned and thrashed. Maybe it was real, maybe fake. No, it was real. There is nothing more exciting to a woman than a hard, passionate fuck from a man in full possession of himself and about whom she knows little but with whom she is infatuated. It's not only women, though, who can fake passion: so can men. I groaned loudly as she blew me and when I came, I called out her name. She cried out in ecstasy. We both came together, an unusual occurrence for me. Usually I cum alone. Cumming with another wasn't all that it is trumped up to be. She lay in my arms, gazing up at me with hopeful wonder. I found this annoying. An older woman would have sat up on the edge of the bed to smoke a cigarette, gaze uncertainly at herself in the mirror. This I would have preferred. Maybe Adelphi saw visions of a house with a yard, swings, a childishly colored jungle gym and some little thing with ringlets and chubby thighs stumbling around on the grass, leaving behind the effluvium of her shit-loaded diapers.

Adelphi couldn't see the real me; she hadn't yet had time to take full note of the lint on my lapels, the unclipped toenails, the irregularities of my five o'clock shadow, the red scalp rash from the bad dye job, the dandruff hailing from my garments. Human fantasy photoshops the object of endearment into a flawless professional headshot. Still, I kept some part of my reason intact, or so I thought. Again, I knew nothing about Adelphi (and didn't want to know), beyond that she was the anti-Lena, the non-Lena, the Israeli photo negative of my lost love. Each pelvic thrust into her felt like an icepick stabbed into Lena's disloyal married heart.

For a week I slept with Adelphi and mourned Lena, hid my deep sadness well, faking passion every night. What I attained, time and again, was more akin to relief than pleasure. I fed at her body like a wolf gnawing at a days-old kill.

When I thought of Lena I saw her in silhouette, like a figure in a mysterious painting, glimpsed from behind, face turned away, her lithe, delicate figure, the long brown hair falling down her back, her hidden menacing eyes gazing into a distance, unknowable, unreadable, and I wanted, desperately, for her to turn, face me, see me; but knowing with deep despair that she never would, I arose in the middle of the night as Adelphi beside me slept the deep sleep of the young. I retreated to an armchair, to stare into the hotel room's unfamiliar darkness, feeling as I imagine an astronaut might who peers through the porthole of his space capsule into pitch-black unknowable space, inviting awe, but realizing instead that he is little more than a worthless speck of spoiling meat in the immense black trash can of the universe. I knew several now-dead junkies who had come to that conclusion without ever leaving the gutter. But at least they knew, sensed, their journey's time to be brief; whereas mine seemed like it would last for a lifetime, that I would never return to the void from which, evidently, I came.

Realizing that I would always grieve Lena made me want to end it all right then. I clung to the prospect of impersonal sensual pleasure with Adelphi, though I knew that even that was a lie of sorts; pleasure with her was also psychological, an illusion of power, of control, the old over the young, the corrupter over the corrupted, the lost over the clueless, the destroyed over the healthy. What in us wants to devour spring, cause the blossoms to fall, spread illness? What in us wants to defile the virginal? Perhaps it hearkens back to pagan times, the offering up of virgins to the Minotaur. Yet, how ridiculous to think that I could corrupt her—at every moment of our time together, Adelphi was maneuvering with the ingenuity of a first-rate military tactician.

To her, emotions and sex were ammunition. Intuiting the powerful hold of fellatio on me, she fellated me constantly with kittenish mewling sounds, as though a helpless puerile prisoner of my cock, sometimes sucking for as long as an hour, which was far too long, and occasionally, with a heavy-hearted sigh, I stopped her; I tenderly ran my fingertips behind her ear to stroke the soft skin there, and caressed her hair as I gently pushed her off. She'd look at me with wounded surprise. "But I want to," she'd protest in a tremulously disappointed voice. "I want to." Of course, I let her go on, poor thing.

Noting my response to the cock-stiffening contrast of thigh-length black stockings and high heels against her white curved naked body, she wore them during sex, even fell asleep in them, as I slowly ran the sole of my naked foot over the black smooth leather and my fingers hissed over the silk stockings. Sensing the extent to which my mind and affections lay elsewhere she began to talk constantly of love; told me every five minutes that she loved me, wanted to spend the rest of her life with me, to which, sagely, I would reply that, surely, she could not be serious. Having read my latest book she must realize that in romantic matters I am a complete disaster—have never been able to successfully form a union with anyone that lasted longer than a few months at most, and even those all crashed and burned. A hurt, slightly angry bolt would flash through her fantastic green eyes, followed by a pathetically obvious imitation of a look of innocent wonder, and she'd argue, gently smiling, that no, to the contrary, my last book gave her the impression of a divinely sensitive man with an enormous capacity for affection, an assessment that caused me to chuckle, which must have stung her.

Then, the gentle smile vanished as her eyes struggled to contain the hopeful worlds that came crashing down in them. At such times she looked like a pathologically embittered child from desperately impoverished beginnings, a slum orphan who would violently reject any attempt to embrace and comfort her. Over the course of the week I began to notice another Adelphi, one glimpsed when she did not know that I was looking: a ruthless, self-absorbed face, a certain look of soulless cruelty in those green eyes—an Adelphi who could just as soon shove you in front of a Merkava tank as light your cigarette, and it was all the same to her.

Once though, she read aloud a passage to me from my last book in which she claimed to see absolute proof of my human goodness. I felt warmly towards her then.

"But sweetheart," I laughed, delighted. "If anything, that describes a middle-aged ruined paramour finding his pleasure as he can in the final suicidal decade of a completely debauched life."

"What is a paramour?" she asked, face fallen.

"Forget it," I smiled, perching her chin on my fist, like Ronald Colman in one of his thirties flicks, lifting her face slightly to meet her eyes in which I imagined I would see the tender disillusionment of youth but met there instead the gunmetal of cold hatred.

A few days later I texted to Adelphi that I wanted "a break," needed "space"—all the typical euphemistic jargon deployed these days to signal "I don't want to ever see you again." We would get back in touch when I "feel ready"—something I had no intention of doing.

She texted right back that first we should talk. I declined. She begged for a face to face. No, I replied. She left a hysterically crying plea to meet for coffee on Shenken Street. I relented. We met that evening in a café. The waiter, a tall sallow-looking gentleman with a dragoon moustache took our order of two Turkish coffees and turned away to fetch them when I changed my mind and asked him to bring me black tea instead; realizing at that instant that the conversation with Adelphi, who looked a wreck, was potentially explosive I did not want to operate from a position of over-stimulated nerves. My eyes scavenged for serenity in the paisley pattern of the waiter's olive colored shirt.

"So?" I said, trying to make my voice sound paisley. "You wanted to talk?"

"I want us to stay together. I think we make a great couple."

"We aren't a couple. I hardly know you."

"Let's go back to your place. Let's be alone. I miss your cock."

I laughed. "That's a first. No, not a good idea."

Tears. I waited. They stopped. "Here," I said, extending a paper napkin from the dispenser on the table. She refused it, rifled in her backpack, pulled out a crumpled clot of used tissues, buried her nose, blew, wiped, returned the snotty mess to her backpack. She looked at me with a moist, dead stare. At that moment I thought that to bed her now would be like fucking a corpse.

I took her home.

During sex she demanded that I slap her. "I'm a bitch!" she hissed. "Hit the crazy bitch! I know you want to!"

I didn't. But she insisted.

I slapped her.

"HARDER!"

I struck her again.

"AGAIN!" she insisted.

I pulled out. "No," I said, rising from the bed, utterly revolted.

I retreated into the bathroom, in the mirror gaped at my reflection. "Who are you?" I asked it, already knowing after years of such moments that no answer exists, for at any given time you are as you are doing, and very often it makes no sense at all and says nothing whatever about you except that at that particular instant whatever you're up to seems like the only available option, and because we must act, must do something, anything, this is what you are doing, this is what you do, this is what you've become, this is who you are. And it may very well be disgusting. Just then, it was.

"Come back," she called.

I have always preferred to act, even to act badly, than to allow life to reduce me to inaction, do nothing at all. I am no Yogi or Zen monk, would rather die at sea fighting off circling sharks with a length of jagged-edged driftwood from my burning craft than pass away in bed surrounded by whispering strangers in white uniforms, gazing down upon my death rattling form, their pitying looks mingling with little burps of acid reflux from the hospital's vending machine Danishes.

I looked again into the mirror at the reflection of my own demented eyes: "She has to go." I switched off the bathroom light, emerged, lay down alongside her back, propped on my elbow, placed a hand on her shoulder, said, "It's no good. I'm in love with someone else."

"The Berlin woman," she snarled from the pillow.

"Yes."

She jumped to her feet, threw open the door, ran naked into the corridor, slammed the door shut, locking herself out. I heard the corridor window thrown open. Suicide attempt.

She leaned far out, shouted into the street, "You're an emotional criminal! You think you can play people like a yo-yo and do anything you like, but not me, Asshole! Asshole! Not me!"

"Okay," I said, turning to reenter my room. "I'm going to dress and leave. Feel free to trash the place or go, as you like. Or kill yourself if you want. That's your business. But I'm going!"

I stepped in. She flew in behind me, naked, grappling with my elbows, trying to restrain me. "No! No! No! Please don't go! I just want us to be okay. Please! I love you so much! I want to be with you!!"

Sickened, defeated, I sank into a chair and sat there slumped over my shriveled gonads, appalled, muttering to myself. She kneeled before me with her hands on my knees and looked up supplicatingly into my eyes. Here she was, young, naked, tattooed, begging. Men my age would give an arm for this. At the moment she'd do anything I liked. My mind considered options. Anal? One last hand job for the road? But all I wanted was to leave. Yet, I just couldn't seem to pull away because I was weirdly held hostage to some iron-gripped magnetic field that kept me pinned to the chair.

"You're such a great person," she prattled. "I truly love you and want you."

I looked back down at her, miserably. "But I don't want you."

She screamed. Jumped to her feet. Knocked over a chair. "I'm going to shoot heroin. I'm going to overdose and die." She rushed for the door. I jumped from my chair, grabbed her up in my arms, tried, not very hard, to wrestle her into a tender submission, again like Ronald Colman. She squirmed away, ran into the bathroom, locked the door.

Finally, in a fit of disgusted rage I put my shoulder to the door and splintered it, just to show that I could, and as she screamed out for the police I dressed hurriedly and ran away, like some kind of criminal.

Chapter 28

When I returned to the hotel hours later, she had left open the door to my room. The front desk told me that the police had come but that she was gone by then. Would I mind calling them? And, there would be a fee for the door's repair attached to my hotel bill.

"Did she do it?" the front desk manager asked with a look of sympathy. "She seems," he said, "like a very excitable young lady."

"No, in fact, I did it," I answered.

"Oh," he said, nodding with a sad smile. "The damage was not extensive, really," he explained. "Only the frame."

"I'm sorry for the trouble," I said.

"Not at all," he said. "These things happen."

"Yes," I said, "apparently they do."

"Affairs of the heart," said the manager. He shook his head sadly.

"They are very difficult for me," I said.

He smiled with chagrin. "For all of us." And added, "My friend, not to worry. We'll give you a new room until your door is fixed."

I thanked him. "I'll just stay in the new one," I said. "No need to switch me back. Charge me if it's extra."

"We have many vacancies," he said. "It's the off-season, you know. You can have any room you like. Same rate as the one you're in."

"It doesn't matter," I told him, "it really doesn't." And this was true. I no longer cared where I stayed, where I awoke or fell asleep or even what city I was in. They were all now matters of indifference to me. And people were alike wherever I went. It was the same unendearingly dull daily aching business going on everywhere, without variation or change. In this way do we live and die. On some table the same cup and saucer. On some night table the same digital clock. In the same night window, the same black featureless view studded with distant anonymous lights. The same passing cars. Some language spoken that one doesn't comprehend or care to. The same damned indecipherable sky. Only painters discern subtle differences of light in nature but apart from them, who really cares about all that? Or about the goddamned charming little towns? Who cares about the same ancient cobblestoned quarters in the center of the same-looking cities? Who gives a good goddamn about boutique shops or castles or paintings or restaurants that are alike everywhere? It's enough to drive one completely insane.

One wants to be a child again. You want someone to take your hand and show you all the wonders to be seen. But no one does. The soul's child-like eyes are caulked shut with stale layers of old feces.

When I called the police, no one knew what I was talking about. Police everywhere are mostly the same: sick to death of civilian disturbance. An Israeli policewoman came on the line. I told her what had happened, then asked, "Well, what should I do?" For a moment I felt a flush of hope that I would be incarcerated in some remote facility for violent offenders. I envisioned crumbling walls, metal toilets, dumb guards in sweat-soaked uniforms. There would be hard labor, bad food, and group therapy sessions with a pretty young social worker who pretended to care, or perhaps really did. It wouldn't matter either way.

"Forget it," said the officer.

I laughed.

"Forget it," she said again, deadpan. She hung up. So many things, places, people, events, conversations, meals, lovemaking, efforts, tasks, feelings, injuries, rewards, achievements, dreams have been dismissed in just such a way, the world an ocean of amnesia. It could be my motto: Forget it!

I did.

But Adelphi didn't make it easy. She called and texted for days and weeks after, unconvinced that I did not really love her, still believing that, somehow, we could yet succeed. The thought of my brief liaison with her sickened me, for after all I had used her, if only for a few days, a week at most, but even during that time, hoping to immerse myself in a sex bath of forgetfulness, all I could think of was Lena, Lena, Lena whom, enigmatically, I still loved, perhaps now more than ever.

So perhaps it was no accident that right after Adelphi's last text, a storm of emails, phone calls, and texts began to rain down on me from Lena, sometimes in the middle of the night, waking me out of a dream, as if she and Adelphi were somehow connected by some feminine routing device, an uncanny sixth-sense uterine network signaling one to the other that now it is her turn.

Half asleep, I'd reach uncomprehending, reflexively, for my buzzing cell phone, check. Lena, writing I love you! Lena, writing I miss you! Writing, I know that you don't want ever to hear from me again, but I want you to know that I don't care who you are with or what you are doing. I love you still. I will always love you."

Sleep, impossible. Night after night I lay awake, awaiting her communications to which I did not reply and could not have if I wanted to. Paralyzed in bed, staring at the ceiling, waiting, perhaps to die. Perhaps if I waited supine for long enough death would simply, quietly, comply, steal over me, shut down my organs one by one, until only breathing was left and that growing shallower and shallower.

Then an email came from her best friend, Tsurah, an Israeli academic philosopher going to waste in Berlin who had attempted suicide on three separate occasions, unsuccessfully of course, and who wrote, "You don't know me, but I know that you know of me. Lena has told you about me. I am Lena's close friend. I am worried about her. She is very much in love with you and unable to bear the possibility that she may never have you. I know that she told you about my suicide attempts. I know what that is, what it looks like, the signs. Lena is close, if not already there . . ." and so on. I rolled on my side in bed, to stare out at darkness, behind me the laptop's glowing ghoulish radiance casting strange shadows on the wall that I realized was me. Whereupon, the harp-like musical notes announcing a Skype message played and a blue square containing Lena's face pinged in the corner of the screen. I slammed the laptop shut, climbed to my feet—hand extended in the lightless room, a blind man wandering lost in strange new surroundings—found a switch, turned it on, winced and staggered to the bathroom to pee, then stood near the hotel room window; I realized with a sinking heart that outside a hard-driving rain battered the streets and window, and looking out on the gray-black silhouettes of wind-tossed trees and an occasional passerby ducking under an inverted and collapsed umbrella, I wondered what lay beyond Death and knew as sure as I have ever known anything that Nothing lay beyond, absolutely Nothing.

Chapter 29

I could not sleep for the rest of the night. I surfed YouTube videos of Hamas firing rockets into southern Israel, Iranian troops training for jihad on Jerusalem, part of a documentary about Ilan Halimi, the young French Jew abducted by Parisian Arabs and tortured to death over twenty-four days. His death became something of a community event, neighbors dropping by to take swipes with a sharp knife at the young boy's flesh. Unable to bear more, I switched to a full-length Israeli film about the famed Entebbe raid, called *Operation Thunderbolt*, starring Yehoram Gaon as Yoni Netenyahu, in which three Lockheed C-130 Hercules-bearing Israeli commandos land on the tarmac of Entebbe Airport in Idi Amin's Uganda and liberate a planeload of Jewish hostages from their Palestinian terrorist captors. I felt calmed by the sight of Israelis with Uzis running through the airport mowing down terrorists. I stared with a sense of awed puzzlement at people who actually cared enough to do something in a crisis. Finally, as the rousing all-male military chorus song played and the credits rolled, I drifted off to sleep, feeling that, at least for now, in my film-opiated brain, justice prevailed, the world was safe; opportunities for heroism and meaning abounded.

And I slept. It had been a long time since I had done so normally. Even before meeting Lena I had been up nights thinking about the new war against the Jews. But since meeting her I thought less about anti-Semitism, more about what exactly did I want from her? I found that I could not name it. Did I want her to make the world feel safe for me again? Did I want Lena all to myself, without Hubert? Yes, certainly: Lena for me and me alone. Lena without Rolf. Lena without her Facebook one-night stands.

But she was in Berlin with Hubert now or with Rolf or both, awake, Skype-texting me as one or the other or someone else unknown to me no doubt slept alongside her or like me lay awake angrily watching her Skype, wondering with whom? I knew that she wanted me but would never leave her little stable in order to be mine and I knew that despite what Hubert had told me they are still together and always would be. I had no place in her comfortable little lie of a life. She could fly to wherever I might happen to be and could even stay with me for a time, play house, pretend that between us exists more than addictive infatuation but in the end she would return to him, always, as she had so many times before, and I began to understand why Rolf had never stayed with her for more than three months in a year: because she would not give him more. Perhaps, as with me, she Skyped him for the other nine months sending her long lonely seductive pleas across the vacuous interstices of the Internet as she waited out the ticking moments of her ever-expiring existence—the same as me, the same as anyone, afraid to be alone.

San Francisco

Chapter 30

I'm on board an airplane bound for New York City, my birth place, city of my youth and young manhood before I moved to Israel. Now I am about to return, homeless, having sold off my pied-à-terre in San Francisco—to many close friends an inconceivably disastrous act.

My assets: moderately well-known mid-list author and editor with over ten published books to my name. The unfulfilled book contract for the book I cannot write: "Masada X." A bag full of clothes. A state of shock.

Lena—hearing from Gerhardt that I was selling off my flat, which would bring me in a large sum of money—in a last-minute reversal cancelled her plans with Rolf, whom she informed me was shattered—and flew to San Francisco to rendezvous with me for my last three months in the Bay Area.

In those months, Lena tore my life to shreds, criticized me constantly, hated all my friends, despised San Francisco, railed against the fog, the Golden Gate Bridge, the price of yogurt, bread, milk, the quality of the kasha sold in local markets, the cost of everything from clothes to movies and when she had me crushed to the point of delirium, persuaded me to leave everything, my whole life, to spend ten days with her in Berlin while she said good-bye to Hubert, then to spend another five months in New York City where she had a fellowship at the Center for Jewish Culture; and after, we'd live elsewhere, maybe Portugal, and use my real estate windfall to purchase a house near Lisbon.

I agreed.

On the day we were to fly off together to our new life, she left me crying on a sidewalk outside the downtown San Francisco Union Square hotel to which we had come to spend the last night before our departure.

In the hotel we had made love. She had wanted me. Twice she drew me onto her, then climbed on top and said, "Come inside. Cum into me." Which I did and soundly slept, holding her nestled in my arms. Maybe we could be happy after all.

Come morning, in the hotel room, still in bed, she reached into her handbag, threw a fistful of cash at me, said, "I'm flying to Berlin alone. Don't come. It's over!" She then hurriedly dressed while I watched, stunned, and she expressionlessly, wordlessly hauled her bags downstairs, and just minutes later, as I stood shocked on the sidewalk she got into a taxi and rode off, not once looking back.

For this woman I had given up a wonderful flat in a city without a single vacancy left in it, said good-bye to innumerable friends, to everything that had come to mean life to me; had discontinued work on "Masada X," the novel I had returned to San Francisco to write but which was struck dead in its tracks by Lena's sudden arrival.

At her insistence, to save money, we had booked tickets for New York on separate flights, our plan to rendezvous in Berlin's Tegel Airport to which our flights were scheduled to arrive just minutes apart. We would then proceed to her flat, which she would pack up, as she had sworn that she was divorcing Hubert, the papers already in process.

After Berlin we would continue to New York where she had the five-month fellowship. Then, off to Lisbon to buy a flat, live together happily ever after, etc.

We would also travel frequently, at her insistence. She could not bear, she had told me, to remain anywhere too long. We would write books, make our way by our wits and pens, but I knew how we would finance all this: the money in my bank account.

No sooner had she come to San Francisco than trouble began. She was a brutal bully who dictated how I would dress, what I would eat, what I would do, when I would do it; what I would think, read, say, feel, and want. She criticized me from morning to night and as always kept in constant touch with other men, scores of them, on Skype, Facebook, SMS, telephone, and social media platforms in German and Ukrainian that I didn't even know existed, all of which made me insanely jealous and frighteningly insecure.

She finagled on her iPad obsessively at all hours of the day and night.

"What are you doing?" I mumbled, woken up by the sound of her typing fingers drumming on the tablet's surface.

"Writing," she snapped, face uplifted eerily in the dark room from the tablet in her lap. It was digital water torture of my brain. Literally, at 3 a.m. in bed she was punching out text right next to my ear and was still at it the following afternoon and on and on into the early morning hours. No rest, no sleep. Jealousy snaked my chest, secreted black foulness. My suspicions grew obsessive. Was she communicating with Rolf? She had thousands of male friends on social media who gushed about her great beauty. One even used her photo as his own profile picture. "Who is that?" I asked her? "No one. That's Wolfie. A pathetic musician. You're so jealous. You need to be on medications!"

I felt like a downed pilot held captive in North Korea, hallucinating with exhaustion, brainwashed to believe patently absurd lies. My pleas to moderate her bedtime writing met with snarls. I stumbled through the days crazed, exhausted. Never had I met someone so arrogant or boastful. She made frequent allusions to her desire that we switch out genders, she to be the man, I the woman. Often, she clamped her fingers over my nipples, crushed them painfully, and then bit into them with her teeth, pretending to suck, as though breastfeeding. The pain was staggering.

I began, by slow degrees, to slip into a submissive subordinate role. She made jokes about putting me into a dress, wondered aloud how I'd look in a wig. She had absolutely no respect for my opinion about anything whatsoever, derided my views, my writing, appearance, hygiene, friends, interests, apartment, and so forth. I wept furiously. At times she drilled me about my experiences in the Israeli army. Had I killed anyone? Yes? No? I had but that was none of her business, so I said no, and she jeered, "No? What kind of soldier are you? Not even a real soldier! Real soldiers kill their enemies!"

She started up again the campaign to get me to pee sitting down, Euro-style, but if I wasn't going to do so in Berlin, I'd be damned if I would do so in America. We had knock-down drag-out fights over this crap. She actually shoved me as I stood in the bathroom over the bowl urinating. I ended up spraying the wall. She shrieked, "THAT IS WHAT YOU DO AT NIGHT WHEN YOU GET UP TO PISS AND STAND THERE IN THE DARK! NOW YOU CLEAN IT UP!!" Not a single action I performed escaped her disdain. During the first week in San Francisco, as I stood in the bathroom before the mirror, shaving, she snatched up a pair of barber scissors that I kept to trim my goatee, and grabbing the back of my long hair chopped it off. For that alone I should have punched her in her insolent mouth and sent her back on Lufthansa but instead, never one to lift his hand to a woman, I stood gaping at myself in the mirror with an amazed and sickened smile, dreading to meet her eyes, see the expression on her face.

What sort of mad person would do such a thing? I felt raped and was reminded of my first time together with her, when she thrust her hand down my pants and clasped my cock, despite my objection and request to take it more slowly; how she tugged at it and squeezed painfully, trying to milk a rise from it that she could ride and when that failed just climbed aboard anyway, stuffed the soft shocked cock into her wet cunt and grinded away until she came.

It took visits to two different hair stylists to straighten out the chop suey mess she had made; and, of course, I now looked completely different, not at all like myself. I gaped at the face in the mirror: who is that? She attacked my wardrobe too, went through my closet and began tossing out shoes, shirts, ties, hats, pants, briefs, socks, tee shirts, coats, jackets, scarves. Nothing I wore worked for her. I watched three-quarters of my closet vanish into black garbage bags which she hauled down to the street and left on various street corners for the homeless to take. For days after I'd see the contents of the bags strewn about in the gutters of my hood. Now and then I saw some homeless gent wearing my favorite sports jacket, shirt, sweater, or hat and felt jealous of their homeless freedom.

When we'd met at the festival in Austria, she had attended my reading and after told me that she thought me a genius. But now, in San Francisco, she called me an antiquated literary flop, my subjects too narrow, my ignorance of philosophy and of avant-garde esthetic concepts so vast that she did not feel able even to attempt an intelligent conversation. Every other word from her mouth was about Barthes, Pascal, or Bergounioux. "Do you even know what "Extrême Contemporain" is?" she'd sneer at me over kasha. We ate kasha three times a day, the only thing she deigned to cook. Kasha mixed with sardines. Kasha with broccoli. Kasha with kasha. I paid every time we went to a restaurant or movie or on a trip or at the supermarket. But when we returned home, rather than saying thank you or, even better, nothing, she launched into long tirades against my destructive spending habits. To her, my purchases at the supermarket, of, say, chicken breasts, quilted toilet paper, grapes, and Chock Full o' Nuts instant coffee stank of elitist capitalist depravity. Each dollar spent in America was a dollar less towards the apartment she intended to purchase someday near Lisbon. Until then, we were to subsist on soup made with weeds picked from parking lots and laden with chunks of stewed rat.

Chapter 31

San Francisco is one of the most beautiful cities in America. But seeing it through Lena's eyes made it painfully ugly to me, unbearable, uninhabitable. Traveling with her on buses through the city was like touring Dante's *Inferno*, with poor people transformed into monsters undeserving of pity or even of Life, the buses themselves rolling cattle cars packed with fodder for the oligarchic charnel house. She detested diners, despised cafés, found the parks dull; the Pacific Ocean was a "disappointment." San Francisco had the worst zoo she had ever seen. She window-shopped in Union Square and on Haight Street with cold disbelief at how stupid, vulgar, and overpriced she found it all. American women were "morons." American men were "child-men." The only thing American of which she approved unreservedly was the dogs. To walk on any street with her was to stop several times on a single block to converse with a dog—not the dog owner, whom she roundly ignored—but the dog. She spoke to dogs, petted them, exclaimed with glee when they shat or pissed. She would actually stop to watch a dog defecate, its rear legs trembling and tail lifted, a long brown cylindrical turd expressing from its dilating red anus, and gasp, "How beautiful!" She also relished the stench of dog feces, inhaled it with a look of opiated pleasure. She stood in dog parks among the scurrying curs with a dazed look of happiness. But she would never actually consider owning one, she said, because they are a "pain in the ass" to care for. You had to walk them three times daily. She had no time for that. What would she do when she traveled to India which she had to do at least once a year? I said, "It can't be harder than taking in tow some lover to fuck."

She glared. "A dog would be easier to care for than you," she said.

She did not approve of movies, did not watch them. If, after days and nights of pleading, I succeeded to drag her from home to go see one, invariably about halfway through she demanded that we leave. If I refused, she just walked out. Once one of my favorite pastimes, I stopped going to film houses altogether. She sat glaring at restaurant menus with imperious indignation, reading the prices aloud, demanding that we go elsewhere. When I insisted we stay, pleaded with her to give the food a try, and reminded her that I would cover the bill, she picked at the served dish with an expression of furious disgust. As she ate, she checked her cell phone constantly, scrolling through messages from who knows where? Never did I feel that I was the only person in her view at any given moment; I felt, rather, that I was an impediment to something else she'd rather do, someone else she'd rather see. She ridiculed every single friend whom I introduced her to. One was a mediocrity. Another was a neurotic mess. So and so was a self-absorbed asshole. Yet another made her feel sick just to look at. Every kindness offered by these, my closest and dearest friends, was met with a lip-curled imperious rejection. About each one of my closest and dearest friends, she said, "I never want to meet that person ever again!"

Yet, crazily, despite these and other horrors, I continued to love her. I dreaded being abandoned by her, which she threatened nearly every day. Sometimes she packed her bags and pretended to leave. I'd block the door. Push her back onto the bed. Pin her down. Fall to my knees. Plead. Beg. Crawl into a corner and hide there, hugging myself as she went to the door, opened it, seemed about to step out, then slammed it shut in disgust and sneered, "I hate you. I'm sick of you! But I can't."

Never have I experienced as much abandonment of myself as during such episodes. What did I fear to lose? I didn't know but it felt like the world would end. That dread lodged like biting snakes in the pit of my being, the very core, where the chest meets the abdomen, and in my pressurized skull, all flowed together into a liquid scream sliding through every blood vessel and neurotransmitter in my incinerating brain.

Sometimes, at night, when unable to sleep, I left her there on the bed tapping away at her tablet. Going into my study I took out the notebooks in which I had begun to compose "Masada X" and read.

One night I tore it all up, realized it was the wrong story. There was another tale that I had been born to write. It would be a fictionalized account of Meir Har-Zion, an actual figure from the Israeli past, a man's man, a lion, once regarded as Israel's greatest soldier.

Night after night I composed, sometimes for an hour or two, other times for fifteen minutes only. Still, my pen moved with confidence, knew exactly the story it had to tell. From the depths of my humiliation Har-Zion stepped forward to be what I never would.

The story opens in 1949, one year after Israel's truly miraculous War of Independence when, despite the onslaught of seven Arab armies comprised of well-armed, highly trained troops numbering in the hundreds of thousands, the tiny, fledgling, and poorly equipped army of the Jewish state, the Israel Defense Forces, succeeded to repel the invaders and to win the war.

But now, one year later, 1950, having suffered heavy losses, the troops are gun-shy, wary of combat, do all they can to avoid skirmishes. On three sides of the Jewish state, from across the fenceless borders pour hordes of marauders, from Egypt's Gaza, from Jordan, and from Syria, huge armed bands of renegades bent upon rapine and mayhem.

They abduct young Israeli women at work in the fields of the kibbutzim, drag them into the desert, rape and torture them, cut off their heads, hands, and feet, then dump the mutilated corpses at the edge of the field and melt away across the border.

They invade some of the more exposed border hamlets, break into homes, murder everyone inside, and are particularly intent upon capturing and tormenting women and children so as to drive terror into the hearts of the Jewish population; to a great extent their plan succeeds. Israelis begin to regard the outer dark beyond the border as an impenetrable black unknown in which lurks horrors beyond imagining. They begin to feel claustrophobic, depressed, dejected, demoralized—their tiny land of liberation becomes a prison fraught with threat. Something like the way I now felt cohabiting with Lena.

On a border moshav, or private collective farm, seventeen-year-old Har-Zion is asked his age by a young girl named Judith, who wonders if he can navigate on foot, without aid of a map or compass, all the way to the mysterious Jordanian archeological site of Petra, an actual city carved from the red stone of a hidden valley and one of the wonders of the world.

Calmly, Har-Zion answers that he can. She dares him to do it and he accepts. She demands that he take her along with him. That night, off they go, on foot, bearing small parcels of food, the young Har-Zion armed with a British-make five-shot .38 Webley slung from a hip holster, and dangling from his gun belt a Huarti, those little knives used by Bedouin hunters to slit the throats of game birds.

Through the night they walk and they sleep by day, hidden among rocks and in wadis. They slip past border guards, traveling through regions patrolled by some of the most terrifying of the Arab murder gangs. On the third day they reach Petra, tour its wonders, and fill their pockets with samples of the red rock to keep as souvenirs.

When Har-Zion and Judith reach home they find the farm in turmoil, worried that they had been abducted and spirited off into Jordan. When the relieved but furious farmers demand to know where the hell he and Judith have been, Har-Zion reaches into his pocket, removes a red stone, lays it on the table. One of the farmers, an amateur archeologist (as were most Israelis then) picks up the stone, turns it this way and that, and says, astonished, "This is from Petra. He has been to Petra."

"Is it true?" the astonished farmers demanded. "You have been to Petra?"

All he did was nod. Then he rose and walked off to his cottage to lie down for a nap. This was how Har-Zion became known throughout the land of Israel as a man of great deeds but few words.

News of his extraordinary feat spread throughout the kibbutzim and moshavim and thence into the towns and cities. Har-Zion became nationally famous, a young hero who had broken the black spell of fear that had held an entire nation captive. Soon, other young Israelis attempted to emulate his feat. Sadly, most were killed.

When he turned eighteen, he entered the IDF where he was regarded as too gifted to serve in a mere combat unit. Instead he was assigned to the newly formed Kilometer 101 commando group, an elite squad under the command of young Arik (Ariel) Sharon, which was so secret that they were permitted to dispense with all military formalities, even the standard uniforms and regulation arms, and could dress as they pleased and outfit themselves with whatever weapons they chose. Most dressed in khaki shirts, shorts, and hiking boots and carried Russian-make Kalashnikovs taken from the corpses of raiders. Har-Zion carried one and an American-make Colt .44 automatic pistol. They all wore Arab keffiyeh for scarves, excellent for shielding against the sun and covering the face in a dust storm. For their eyes they wore goggles. They ranged by jeep, making lightening raids into the territories held by the marauders. Widely feared, they were ruthless in their reprisals.

In this atmosphere, Har-Zion, a natural scout and fighter, thrived. At a very young age, less than twenty-two, he attained the rank of captain.

And so he should have remained, always to be renowned for his trek to Petra but otherwise destined to live out his days like any soldier and end his life either on the battlefield or in retirement on an agricultural settlement.

Fate, however, had other plans in store for him.

New York City

Chapter 32

On our last morning in San Francisco, as we lay abed, postcoital, in a Union Square hotel, hours away from flying to Berlin after which we were to spend five months in New York—after I had already sold off my pied-à-terre in a hurry for under-market rate, given away everything I owned, bid good-bye to friends of years and to the one city outside Tel Aviv that had been my base of operations for over a decade—suddenly, unaccountably, she threw a fistful of money on my chest—the price of my airline ticket—and said that she was going to Berlin without me. "Don't come," she said. She wanted never to see me ever again. And as I lay there in utter shock, Lena rose, dressed, took her bags, slammed the door, went downstairs, hailed a cab, loaded in her bags, rode off, left me behind shattered on the sidewalk. She never once looked back.

I remained in the hotel for a week, alone, had a kind of nervous breakdown, talking to walls at three o'clock in the morning, gibbering at my own reflection in the bathroom mirror, pulling out my hair, rolling fetally curled from side to side in the bed, moaning; and after a week of this I decided that I must go to New York City, could not remain in San Francisco. Suddenly, I was futureless. Suddenly, I was homeless.

My first morning in New York, I awoke shocked, disoriented, in a tiny frozen room on a disheveled bed in the home-cum-museum of my friend, the photographer Caleb Matheson, afraid to think of Lena, or of what to do next, how to proceed, recoiling before so much concrete proof of my mental and social predicament. It lay all around me and within me. Every step made in Manhattan confirmed that life as I had known it was gone while the Berlin woman whom I gave it all up for was probably fucking Rolf or someone else, some Wolfie or Reinhardt or something. Just going to the corner bodega to buy mealy bagels and Tropicana orange juice required agonizing effort.

My mind reeled at what she had done. How could I have allowed this to happen to me? I, who had always been so careful to take only the most calculated risks, who feared heights and avoided cliffs and high windows? How would I trust myself ever again? I had thrown myself over a cliff, jumped off a roof. I was falling, plummeting, consciously, horribly. How would I survive this disaster? Why was I not at home, in my bed? Who was this aging man, this fetal fallen man, abed in an unheated wintry room, shivering in my skin? Was this me? I felt no real sense of self, beyond the flicker of a tearstained reflection peering from a cave of defeat in a tiny wall mirror, while outside, the fiery meteors of world's end were falling, the wind drumming, the sabertooth roaring, and a war party of cannibal Neanderthals fast approaching, in their nostrils my scent.

I felt not like an author, known to readers and other writers. Not like a celebrated literary man. Not as though I had, in actuality, close to a half-million dollars in my bank account but like someone flat broke, abandoned, the dirty animal she often told me that I was, a last remaining dinosaur awakened to my own extinction. During our time together, she would go on and on about some other writer or artist who was in her estimation a great genius, while I fell further and further down into the bottomless pit of her inexhaustible disdain. She would scold about how irrelevant I am, that I must change my tack, be more like those others whose names she uttered with reverence—all Russians or Germans whose names I can't recall. You and your Holocaust, she would jeer, you and your Israel! No one wants to hear about that syrupy shit anymore. "Jews, Jews, Jews!" she—herself Jewish— would chant with distaste. She could not bear my mentioning Israel a single time more. In Berlin, she said, it was Holocaust this and Hitler that. Enough already! I must, she had demanded, think differently, dress differently, write differently, be anything but who I am, what I am, not a Jew who writes about Jews but an internationalist who explores and celebrates racial exotica. "That is what your neoliberals want to read about! The Eskimos! The Polynesians! The Bamba of Uganda!" I must be anything but what I had fought so hard to become: a Jewish author.

She mocked, too, my recovery as the child of a survivor and belittled the support groups I occasionally attended. I will be your recovery, she had said, her voice mannishly hard. But that is impossible, I said; you're not God. And besides, you should be glad that I'm so dedicated to becoming sane. If it weren't for those meetings, I would go mad.

Never, she'd snarl. You'll never lose your mind! I'm sure of it. There's no guarantee, I said. I can't survive by myself. I need support. And I need to help others. It's the only way to keep the gift of life. She greeted this with scorn as thunderous as when I once mentioned my belief that some kind of God was watching over me. What New Age bullshit! You're such a weak liberal Jew! God? I don't need God, she had snapped. I just need myself. I haven't seen you help anyone besides yourself since I've known you. You're a selfish sex addict who uses the Holocaust to justify your self-indulgence. But I had never found that I alone sufficed, I told her. I was not the strong, silent type, much as I'd once hoped to be. I require people. That's why I give readings, why I tour. I'm socially crippled. I don't know how to connect with others. And not just any kind of people but those who have suffered, who have known extreme loss, failure, pain. I only feel at home with those with mad brains and broken hearts. Sad people hurt by life. Bad drunks always connect with me. Drug addicts. Sure, I told her, you're lucky. You don't seem to need others, though so many loners wind up as gutter suicides. In my youth Hemingway and Kerouac were my role models. Hemingway persuaded everyone around him—he was always in the company of others—that not only did he need no one, but he was better than everyone else. Many believed that and endured his abuse, right until the day he held a loaded shotgun to his paranoid hairline and after a lifetime of warfare, fishing, hunting, womanizing, and literature, discharged one last round beyond the river and into the trees. True to himself as always, he had slain his greatest and most dangerous prey: himself. His own mangled head was his last trophy. It should have been mounted on a wall in the Museum of Natural History, along with the rhinos, lions, boars, leopards, elephants, ibexes, buffalo, and other beasts he slew so joyously. My other idol, Kerouac, was an anxious, giddy, drunken, hapless, sexually confused lover and loner who like Hemingway also traveled in a pack—albeit a pack of Beat loners—yet even among these oddballs he felt different, often saw himself as inferior to those around him; found others intolerable and had to quaff mighty droughts of booze to numb the pain of his own catastrophic social ineptitude.

All crap, she said. You are full of it.

Perhaps I was. In some ways she was right. I could never really run with a pack, try as I might—I was and still am a true loner, perfectly content to wander aloof through long deserts of time, observing my own emotional anguish and mental agitation, recording my memories of dissolution and defeat, transforming the raw notes into book-length texts, memoirs, novels, or poems and stories—or composing long essays aggrieved with the shabby, greedy turn that society has taken, the passivity and incomprehension of youth who seem incapable of passionate response or commitment to anything but their own spell-binding iPhones and flyweight laptops. At such duped, self-aggrandizing adult infants I want to rage, Listen! Have you any notion of the stupendous hoax that has been perpetrated upon you by the carnival barkers of tech? The priestly con men of corporate dreck culture? Do you not see your entire existence sliding into the black maw of your tricky little apps? Do you not see that you are ensnared by an addiction more cunning than crystal meth?

But to whom would I such speeches make? Any small audience I might attract would disagree within minutes of listening to my hoary late-night lament. My voice is not sunny. My dreaming life, made into books, now have a shelf life of their own, live quite well without me. It's all so meaningless to me personally. No book can stop a Hitler, Stalin, Putin, or Trump. Really, sitting here I want to end it all. I am only tears, useless to the world. I wanted to love and be loved, to live richly and fully. Instead, I feared and was ridiculed. Now I am arrived—abandoned, broken, and tired—to the city where I came out screaming from between my mother's bloody thighs, to which I have returned with over ten book titles to my name and sleeping in the tiny room behind Caleb Matheson's Renegade Museum.

Caleb, an old admiring colleague, is a buffalo-sized wild man who photographs the underbelly of Manhattan and has frequent run-ins with cops. Often, he's on the front page of the *Daily News* or the *New York Post*, in handcuffs. When he heard what had happened to me, he offered the tiny room behind his "museum," gratis. "This is not a time when you should be alone," he said. It's actually just a giant firetrap crowded to the ceiling with packrat junk—everything from the naïve art of an alcoholic former fireman to crappy B-run DVDs sent to him by a homicidal maniac doing life upstate for carving up a stripper and serving her as stew to the East Village homeless in Tompkins Square Park.

Piled everywhere are boxes of old newspaper and magazines, and interspersed among them giant sculptures he once fashioned from trash salvaged from the street and soldered together into grotesque shapes, like street tumors of rusted metal excavated from a 1980s time capsule. In other words, he is a hangover from a long-dead punk rock past.

His photos—portraits of East Village trannies, junkies, poets, rockers, punks, gangsters, rabbis, Jehovah's Witnesses, drug dealers, bodega grocers—are important; they contain the whole vibrant and complex fabric of New York's Lower East Side. The problem is, Caleb feels unappreciated. He feels abandoned, alone. His wife, Lola, has dementia and wanders through their Twilight Zone loft like a figure from a Tennessee Williams play, muttering, "Where is Zippy? Have you seen Zippy?"—their dog who died a decade ago. Caleb, overweight, Viking-bearded and wearing a cap emblazoned with a Jolly Rodger, sits parked right outside my door at his computer until four or five in the morning, drumming out endless ranting emails to anyone he can think of, including me, about his neglected career, the mercenary mayor in City Hall, the rapacious realtors who have sterilized the neighborhood, and most of all the shouting belligerent frat bros staggering drunk past his front door like stormtroopers out on the town, accompanied by clones of Miley Cyrus (whom Caleb calls Miley Virus) dressed in crotch-baring tiny skirts and teensy halters bearing the emblem of the Ramones, puking all over his front door and screaming and crying, laughing and screeching, "FUCK YOU YOU!!! YOU WANT A BLOW JOB??? YOU WANT HEAD??? MOTHER-FUCKER!!! FUCK YOU!!! HA HA HEE FUCKING FUCK!"

To see what he puts up with every night, one can't help but empathize. But when he goes on about the "sell-outs" who betrayed the neighborhood (he owns the building in which he lives—a property worth five million—and leased the air rights to the twenty-story gentrifying monster hotel next door) and about the aging and sick former Warhol superstar Maury Tinsel, who was evicted from his squat and died in the streets, I want to ask why he didn't clear away some of the rubbish upstairs to make a little cubbyhole for the old queen, and by the way, don't profitable deals with a giant hotel qualify as gentrification? Is that not selling out? But I hold my peace. After all, I'm living by Caleb rent-free. And I know that his real objective, having heard of my money from the sale of my flat, is to sell me for a small fortune one of his junk-metal CBGB-stylized art atrocities. Because of course, nothing in this world is for free. When I exit from my room, he is there, always there, immense, complaining, a dead ringer for the Norse god Odin, and he's such a gigantic pain in the ass that no one will take a chance on giving him a show or even acquiring the work. The moment anyone displays the least interest in him he raises grand artifices of deluded scenarios in which he is about to "take over the art world," followed by a period of raging and inexplicable resentment of the very people trying to help him and then caps it off by spinning paranoid conspiracies so vast and unintelligible that one would need a detailed interstellar map to encompass the scope and complexity of the sinister forces arrayed against him.

"Hey, Nathan, my man," he calls out softly when I appear. He has set things up so that as I exit from the room even just to pee, I must pass by a ghoulish gallery of his worthless junk art. "You see that piece over there, the robot figure with the pizza shop sign for a mouth? I made that in 1983. Basquiat and Haring were up here, loved it. What do you think?"

"I'm not an art critic," I smiled wanly as I hurried into a trashed toilet covered in a fine silt of plaster dust that has been sitting there, probably, for thirty years. Pinned to the wall is a photograph of William Burroughs, his mouth graffitied over with lipstick.

Caleb's archive of photographs sits unwanted, boxes heaped on files, large mounted scratched blowups stacked against walls, cockroaches everywhere, even the occasional rat, and instead of curators it's his photographic subjects showing up at his door for a handout: bums, freaks, hooligans, lushes, and tracks-scarred junkies with gruesomely bruised and festering abscesses. Now and then realtors visit to make him an offer, which he cunningly declines.

Caleb lets them all in, a slimy leak of garbage-reeking visitors, and shares his drugs and booze, gets wasted, eats greasy fried takeout from the corner bodega, and the days march by in a shivering procession of blown opportunities and personal decline for which, again, Caleb blames the world and everyone, anyone, or anything but himself. An air of crud decay hangs over him, his home, the museum, his wife, wandering around hungry and neglected, Zippy the ghost dog at her heels.

In fact, it is all reflective of the monumental sense of failure on which he thrives and to which he is addicted. For I have the sense, as days pass here, that Caleb has brought me in not only to peddle his outmoded art but as witness to his own downfall about which—overweight, hypertensive, his liver, lungs and kidneys in collapse, his stomach like a nineteenth-century specimen of elephantiasis, chugging beer and sitting stiffly upright with an air of commanding unctuousness at his computer from morning to night—Caleb rages and rails. I won't even bother to transcribe here his rambling arguments, which are convoluted, wrong, and essentially insane. Suffice to say, enduring one of these jeremiads is an ordeal. Any time I step from my door his voice rings out, "Nathan!" And if it's not a sales pitch it's about former New York City Mayor Bloomberg who is to blame for the entropy of the universe itself. The bastard tore the city apart, a new kind of real estate Hitler. A Mussolini of the oligarchic elite.

"But DeBlasio is mayor now," I offer. "Bloomberg's gone."

"It doesn't matter," he scowls. "They're all in on it together."

But he, a great cherubic Santa of a neglected punk-era legendary failure, he is innocent, the bearer of great truths and as pure as the driven coke aligned on a Joey Ramone album cover.

Chapter 33

Then suddenly, incredibly, she reappears.

She calls, texts, emails, begs me to take her back. I have cleaned up the tiny room at Caleb's, replaced the big reeking spring bed with a tidy camping cot from REI, a trust fund baby-favored outfitter on Broadway and Lafayette, tossed out junk piled to the cathedral-high ceiling, inserted an armchair and soft lamp, hung curtains on the barred window which looks out on a tiny backyard facing the rear of a hipster clothing boutique run by a short slender blonde who yaps in a shrieky vocal fry, and on the cot I lie staring at the blank wall, peering into myself, feeling within only a swirling dense mess of confused, disoriented anxiety, grief. I recalled how I had run down after her outside the San Francisco hotel, pleaded on the sidewalk, and, astonished, watched her pull away in the yellow cab; how her face did not once turn to me, how she maintained a hard-staring disciplined face-front as the car merged with traffic and how I wept there on the sidewalk, inconsolable, shocked. Now, at Caleb's, I lifted the cell phone with a long resigned fatalistic exhalation, watched my thumb slowly, suicidally, press the voicemail retrieval key, and listened to her crying message: "Please, forgive me. I love you. Love you so much!! I'll do anything you want. Go anywhere you want." And tears sprang from my eyes. I spoke to her in my thoughts: I do not want to live in Berlin; I don't want to spend months of each year in India or some other third-world slum. I don't want to become an annual poverty tourist. I don't want to hang out with hunger-crazed people with faces painted blue, wildly-colored parrots, male corpses burning on pyres along with their living widows, raped schoolgirls, gangs of molesting men, children with suppurating facial sores, or blind and legless lepers dragging their truncated bodies through the dust of the marketplace. I don't find any of that charming. To be frank, my love, my dear Lena, little on this earth thrills me anymore, whether in North America, Europe, or the rest. I am sick to death of the whole damned thing, the postcard mountains and cliché beaches, the big gray ocean and the vast blue sky. I am sick of the cities and sick of the country, sick of sunrises, and sick of sunsets. I don't give a fuck about ecology. I don't care if the whole first, second, and third world goes up in a great conflagration of plastic-drowned climate change. I find Nature savage and essentially dull. I don't want to travel thousands of miles to observe gorillas in their natural setting. I can just walk down any street in Munich to see golden haired blue-eyed apes in lederhosen. I find human beings to be incomprehensibly stupid, baffling, and a waste of time. What I now mainly admire are the books and art of the past, produced by long-dead people. What I now most admire are moldering libraries. There, the living are silent and the dead speak. Perhaps some day after I am gone one or another of my books will bring an ember of hope to someone who is as fundamentally lost and weary as I now feel. That is the most I can wish for. As for love, it is a filthy lie. There is no such thing. There is only sadistic and deluded self-interest ensnared by its own crude rationalizations.

I am paraphrasing myself in conversation with an imagined Lena. And imagining, at her end, sniffles and sobs, gasps of pain, the occasional meek "okay."

And then—I regret the use here of the awful cliché "as in a dream" but there is no other way, unfortunately, to describe the experience—one day, as in a dream, I heard my own actual voice on the phone speaking to actual Lena as I lay in my tiny room on the little cot in Caleb's Museum of Renegade Art, expressing the very same views and sentiments paraphrased above. I could tell that at best she was only waiting out my triumphant aria of refusal while weeping just as I had imagined she would, and then in a voice of child-like contrition she sniffled, "Okay, but please, please, stay with me. I'll do anything you want. I'm so sorry. I'll go anywhere you ask." And to my astonishment I heard my own voice say, "All right. I forgive you. I love you. Let's go on."

Frederick Douglas wrote, "Find out what any people will quietly submit to and you have the exact measure of the injustice and wrong which will be imposed on them."

I had rushed from the San Francisco hotel half dressed. Stared down the street. Watched her pull away. And then, she was gone, really gone. On that hotel sidewalk my battered self-esteem could do no better than to crumple me like a paper rose trampled by a marching boot. Even now I dread to think of myself collapsed, imploded, sliding down to the sidewalk, back raked by the hotel's graffiti-marred wall, head slumped forward on my chest, unable to bear the feelings unleashed by her desertion. On my face the sun beat down fiercely. A decision had been made; it shattered my very sense of reality. Dead-set to spend the rest of my life with her, I was now torn up at the roots, the very future erased. I didn't know what I was meant to do even in the next hour, for the problem had not existed just minutes ago, the rupture as baldly surprising as sudden death. I had just been murdered, yet lived. As the cab pulled out, she did not glance back at me. Still, to this day, in thought I go over that moment time and again, even dream of it. How she sat staring straight ahead, her recessing silhouette in the cab's rear window disappearing as I bled out on the sidewalk like an amputated limb.

She had decided to truncate my hope, castrate me, and she did so unflinchingly. Just before, in the room, more had occurred than I can bear to reveal, yet I must. Her decision was delivered like a knife thrust. We had made love twice that night, tenderly—our very last time to make love in San Francisco—so there was an elegiac quality to our exertions amid the estranging sterility of the hotel walls, of noises from an alien street piercing an unfamiliar window as we moved in rhythmic union, flesh bonding in fluent exchange, with full knowledge (I had thought) of each other, two against the hostility of loss, the silent fury of destiny angels that brood ashen-winged over the city. During that love-night my soul intoned dirges of good-bye to what, perhaps, should not be lost or bidden farewell—for so far the years of my life had been good to me, even if I had never really felt at home anywhere but more like a hermit nestled in a groove carved out from wild cliffs by unseen hands with the sole purpose of sheltering me, saving my life; by some mysterious force of kindness unbeknownst to me, I had prospered and thrived, perhaps even more than I deserved, perhaps more than I'll ever know again, though internally I lay in a cave, wounded as painfully as Philoctetes by the Holocaust.

For I am exiled, terrified, brokenhearted, and by choice irrevocably self-severed by a cruel heart thief, though, in all fairness, it is I who had summoned her to come back and destroy my life again, which she did and which, as only a fool could have failed to grasp, was inevitable.

I am just that very fool.

One day, they came to Captain Har-Zion with news that the raped and mutilated bodies of his sister, Shoshana, and her boyfriend had been found just inside the border with Jordan. Preliminary evidence indicated that they had entered Jordan on a secret trek, perhaps to reach Petra, had been abducted by a murderous band of Bedouin marauders, put to torments of fire and knife, she raped, and their butchered remains dumped back in Israel, as a message.

On the spot, Har-Zion resigned his captain's commission. At once, he was called into the office of Arik Sharon, Har-Zion's superior officer. There Moshe Dayan, defense minister, the one-eyed legend in a black eye patch, also sat waiting.

"I know what you're planning, Meir," said Dayan.

Har-Zion said nothing.

"I wouldn't be dumb enough to try and stop you. That's not why you've been summoned. I am here to say that I am sorry about what happened to Shoshana. And that I would do exactly what you are going to do, if it was my sister." He looked at Sharon. "So, tell him what we are asking."

Sharon leaned forward on his elbows, said, "I'm not going to offer condolences. I'm going to say that I wish I were going with you. We only want you to have the best chance to make it back alive. This is our offer. The two best men from the unit have already offered to resign. I think you know who they are."

"Go on," said Har-Zion.

"Take them with a jeep and untraceable weapons that we will supply. We also will brief you on all the intelligence we have about the band that killed Shoshana. Go, do what you must, and when you are done, we will be at the border, waiting to get you back across. That is all we ask. You will have twenty-four hours. When you return, you will be immediately reinstated at your current rank."

"Good," is all Har-Zion replied.

What need was there for "thank yous"? None.

He went, with Uri and Dan, the three dressed in unmarked uniforms, bearing weapons taken off marauders in previous raids, traveling in an old British-make army jeep, also unmarked, and they drove across reddish borderlands as the sun set and crossed over the unfenced marker line between the two nations and were met at the other side by machine gun fire from a Jordanian border patrol. The three scurried from the jeep, found an elevation, and counterattacked, firing, dropping, rolling, rising, charging with guns ablaze, tossing hand grenades. Four Jordanian policemen died. A fifth lay gravely wounded on the ground, groaning, pleading for the end, torso torn open from crotch to neck. Har-Zion dispatched him with a gunshot.

They mounted up, drove on, stopping to survey with high-powered American military binoculars the desolate landscape of rocky hills and arid ground. Now it was dusk, the setting sun blood-spreading over the horizon, a red dust storm rising from the East, the full moon sneaking into place. With keffiyehs around their noses and mouths, goggles pulled over their eyes, they continued on into whirling blindness in which they hid, traveling now by coordinates alone to the approximate location of Shoshana's killers, and up ahead saw in muted silhouette a string of armed men in flapping robes trudging heads down, bent under the fierce storm wind, and were in turn spotted. A firefight ensued. Har-Zion, enraged, stormed their line of fire, followed by Dan and Uri spitting hot lead from their automatic weapons. They mowed down four, leaving five who dropped weapons and with arms raised stood in place, dark unreadable faces watching Har-Zion who noted that they were good faces, the profiles of fighters, of killers, fearless, ruthless, bred in the ways of war; this he could forgive. But though there seemed no hint of sadism in their eyes he knew that each had done things to his Shoshana too monstrous to imagine, and this he could not forgive.

He stated more than asked in fluent Arabic—a language he had learned, as had most Moshav Sabras, those born in the Land of Israel and raised to work its soil and fight her fights—"You are from the tribe of Mahmud Ibrahim Qawwali."

One nodded, face otherwise impassive. None showed the least sign of fear, though all knew what was coming.

Har-Zion motioned with his head, an almost imperceptible gesture, at which Dan and Uri stepped behind the men and one by one tied their hands behind their backs.

Then, Har-Zion removed his Huarti knife, the one that he had carried in his youth to Petra, and held it up before each man's eyes before cutting the man's throat from ear to ear with a single deliberate stroke. The men dropped like dolls, one after the other, and bled out, thrashing and gasping as the rocky soil soaked up their blood with surprising absorbency, almost as though drinking it.

Then he stood before the last Bedouin, looked deep into the man's dark brown eyes, which flinched only slightly. "You," he said, lowering the blood-stained knife in his hand. He removed the man's keffiyeh from his head, dipped it in the blood spill of one of the slain on the ground, and then wiped his own knife clean on it. "You will live. You will go back to your tribe." Wrapping the bloody garment around the man's neck and knotting it tightly, he said, stepping back to examine his handiwork. "Take back to them the blood of their brothers, tell of what I have done. Tell them that the brother of the Israeli girl whom they murdered was here." He got into the jeep, followed by Dan and Uri, and they watched as the Bedouin turned, walked off hurriedly, and vanished into the blinding sandstorm. Then they drove back across the border from where they had come and were met by Dayan and Sharon, waiting for them in a civilian automobile.

"Mission accomplished?" asked the sardonic Dayan, his one good eye crinkling.

Har-Zion nodded.

"Go back. You'll be arrested on base. They'll come for you as soon as the news breaks. Don't worry. We're going to keep you out of jail."

The three men were arrested, thrown into jail. But their handlers treated them with the highest respect. Now and then a policeman bent to the ear of one or the other of the three and said, "All honor to you. If it was my sister, I would have done the same."

The matter exploded, became international news. Jordan lodged a formal protest in the United Nations. Even the United States was angry. "We are not living in biblical times," declared the American UN delegate. "International relations cannot survive the rule of an eye for an eye. There must be diplomacy, restraint. We call upon all the parties to refrain from further acts of violence."

Jordan, feeling the need to respond, fired a few forlorn retaliatory artillery salvoes into the wasteland bordering the two states. They landed pointlessly in the middle of nowhere. Ben Gurion, the prime minister of Israel, called Dayan and Sharon into his office. "What the hell happened? Eshkol, the president, that idiot, is publicly calling for Meir's head. I wish he had just one of Meir's balls. Question: did either of you two in any way aid and abet what Meir did?"

Of course, he already knew. But he had to ask. Dayan looked him straight in the eye with his one good sardonic eye and said, "No."

"Good!" declared Ben Gurion, playing along. "So, it was the act of an aggrieved brother. An understandably aggrieved brother, and not a retaliation of the IDF. There will be no trial. There will be an official reprimand. Har-Zion is barred from active duty for thirty days, after which he will be reinstated at full rank and returned to active service. Now get out of here. And tell him David says hello."

Before Dayan and Sharon left the room, Ben Gurion called out,

"Moshe, is it true? What he did? Let the one live to carry a message back? And the message, he really said that?"

"Of course," said Dayan.

"Incredible," said Ben Gurion, moved. "If only I had more of such men!"

Har-Zion, restored to rank, became a national hero. There was no one throughout the land, except for a few politicians, who disagreed with his deed. There was no one, man or woman, who did not say, "Had it been my sister, I would have done the same."

Later, in a battle, he was wounded in the throat so badly that it ended his career. For his service, he received Israel's highest commendation, the Medal of Valor.

He finished out his life raising horses on a moshav which he founded on a hilltop overlooking the region where his sister had been slain and named it Moshav Shoshana, and he never tried to use his great fame for personal gain or run for office or become a pundit. He rarely issued public statements, and he died, alone, largely forgotten and still grieving for Shoshana on the moshav that he had named for her.

Chapter 34

I completed the novel about Har-Zion, which I entitled "Zion Mountain," in under a month and sent it to my agent who read it and found it, he said, astonishing, brilliant, horrible, and in violation of every tenet of political correctness held sacred by the editorial staffs of the major publishing houses.

"We have," he wrote in an email, "a snowball's chance in hell of getting this published. But I'm going to try. 'Zion Mountain' is just too good not to take the shot."

They took the shot. Afterwards, 'Zion Mountain' was acquired by the venerable old firm to whom I was under contract, now a subsidiary of Web Flicks. The book died. On bookstore shelves nationally, it existed for exactly three months. The returns were huge. It was quickly remaindered. All told, it received five reviews—one of them, on the front page of a national newspaper, found it disgusting but brilliant. And though issued in a British edition, it was never translated, not even in Israel which did not seem to want to know of its existence.

Now, there is nothing. Now I sit in a bookstore-café called Housing Works in the Soho District of Lower Manhattan, in the final thawing days of departing winter and awakening spring, brokenhearted, remembering her and afraid, so afraid of this titanic cruel empty rich man's town, feeling everything, though it is not of my own pain that I sit internally weeping but of her figure in the snow, that deceptively sweet face, head wrapped in a dark shawl and overcoat, snow falling on her slender shoulders, on me, on everything, on that street on the Lower East Side where, finally, I had the fortitude to say good-bye forever, and she looked so pretty but so much, too, like some wan refugee newly arrived to where Jewish ancestors had disembarked from Ellis Island and made their faltering way, her pale, wan face so thin, worn out from protracted suffering; for I have no doubt that, despite her deception and machinations, she, too, suffered. Her anguished tears appeared, felt quite real, though also I've been warned repeatedly that one who displays her brand of sociopathic symptomology is capable of persuasive emotion but incapable of true remorse or actual conscience. But then, how could she? She who came from the Bloodlands of Hitler and Stalin? Virtually identical to a relative killed at Babi Yar, she was, in a sense, like me, born dead.

I don't know what I'm trying to prove, to myself, to anyone, who might someday discover this account but my heart is charred, like the roof and interior of the famed Burnt House in the Old City of Jerusalem, unearthed intact—only the top beams scorched black by fires set when Roman legionnaires raced with swords and torches through the Upper City, hacking and burning everything, slaughtering pitilessly—a massacre gruesomely depicted in *The Jewish War*, an account of the Roman siege of Jerusalem composed by the captured Jewish general Josephus as a warning to neighboring Alexandria of what would happen if they dared, like the Jews, to revolt.

When archeologists peeled away the charred outer skin of the Jerusalem roof beams, they found pink new wood underneath and discovered, inside, on a short flight of steps, a single skeletal arm clutching a spear. Evidently, the roof had collapsed on an armed servant girl who sought escape just as fiery beams collapsed on top of her. Yet, over centuries, the spear remained in her skeletal hand. So my charred heart will remain amidst the ruins of Lena and me.

Sadness, disorientation, and fear globalized—such is what I feel even now, and all through the day when I pull out my cell phone several times an hour to see if she has sent an email, or I check the mailbox repeatedly for a letter from her or gaze out my window at Nothing. The World. Why would she try to reach me now? I've made quite clear my determination never to see her again. But it is the thought of her out there somewhere that stalks me . . . the possibility, so effortless really, that she might make some small attempt to see me once more and that I will, insanely, take her back. I both want to and dread to make love to her, and crave it more even than death, for no dead person suffers in death—as I have through knowing her, with her brutal efforts to reconstruct me into some kind of Frankenstein composite of all the husbands or lovers who had failed to please her impossible personality over decades of unhappy life. And during our time together I wrote next to nothing, experienced a gradual deterioration of my creative resolve, the ruin of my talent, the decimation—as with hand grenades and sledgehammers—of my inward citadel of Life, a bulwark of procreative and artistic urges that I had erected over years of hard-won self-discipline, brick by brick, word by word—huge cleverly plotted linguistic canvasses of sublimated Holocaust themes, loaded with charcoal phantoms, smudged disintegrating faces, and landscapes of incandescent fire—in which voices came and went like shades, characters opened at dusk and folded at dawn like tragedized blossoms, faces blurred in and out of the narrative. But though those books were highly acclaimed, she, with demonic determination, like one possessed, laid siege to my self-esteem with large daily doses of relentless disdain until I began to doubt my worth and gave up altogether on writing, resigned to seeing my books fade from view, forgotten masterpieces consigned by their own author to perish.

There was something of a woman's concentration camp guard in her manner as she supervised the brushing of my teeth for the fourth time that day. She crept stealthily up behind me with a large pair of shears, and with a sudden thrust, grabbed a handful of my long, black hair and lopped it off. No discussion, warning, requested permission, or reason given; she just scissored it off as I stood transfixed with the razor paused at my lower lip, unable to grasp what had just occurred. My mind/heart stood still. I was unable, or unwilling, to move in any direction for fear that doing so would in some way force me to direct my eyes down to the toilet bowl, to the huge pile of black hair that she had just tossed in, her look grimly satisfied, as though some incredibly challenging goal had just been reached. This happened when she had been but a few days in my home. I should have tossed her out right then and there, like a handful of hair. But I could not. She had only just arrived. I hardly knew her, really. Her presumption was so inexplicable that I could barely grasp what had just occurred. It wasn't the first violation either. There had been so many. In Berlin, her hand shooting down my pants. Bursting into the bathroom as I stood urinating and demanding that I pee sitting. Grabbing spoons, forks, combs, pens, books, shirts, socks, soap, out of my hand with a jeering insistence that I stop, stop right now, and do something else, something she wanted. I moved from shock to shock, obedience to obedience. With her, it was always like that. It would take me weeks, months, to absorb something she had done. Like when she told me one night, after swearing up and down that she would get a divorce, that she would never divorce Hubert. The shock was to me so great that I had to leave my own home for nearly an entire night, wandering around San Francisco in the fog, in a state of disorientation, disbelief, unreality. I ended up in Chinatown at three o'clock in the morning, talking on my cell phone to a friend, Eric, a psychologist who had lost a young wife to leukemia, and who listened now so patiently as I wept and raged, and then, quietly, gently, Eric said, "You need to extricate yourself from this person. This is not the first time you've called me about her in a state of distress. You don't deserve to be treated this way. Can't you see that she is breaking your heart?"

"I do. But I don't. I . . . I'm confused. I can't seem to get a purchase on any of it. It's all so painful, so unreal."

"But it's real. And she is really bad for you. She may even be a good person (though I doubt it) but regardless, you need to separate from her completely."

"I don't think I can bear the loss. I don't know why. I've never felt so stuck before in my life. What did you do when your lovely wife died?"

There was a pause that made me instantly regret the question. But he was very kind; he drew a sharp breath, exhaled.

"I'm sorry," I blurted out. "I shouldn't have brought that up."

"That's all right," he said. "It's all right. It's not like I don't think about her day and night. Sometimes I take it minute by minute. Sometimes it's like that. Like I don't want to live any-more. But I tell you, no matter how badly you feel right now, it will pass, and suicide . . . that's not a solution, that's an execution. Who made you judge and jury? And anyway, it just takes one little shift in the wind and the whole world changes, just like that."

I had had so much hope—too much; I felt that I must love her very much, and she, I, or else why suddenly was she there in my home, behind me in the bathroom bending over the toilet flushing down a fistful of my hair? Was not this an act of misguided love, well intended, on her part? An effort to improve me that would be of ultimate, if mysterious, benefit, in ways I could not yet foresee? Though what that might be I could not imagine, and why, after all, was I, as is, inadequate for her? Had she not fallen in love with me, as I was, back in Austria at the festival? Yet the moment I set foot in her home in Berlin the revisionist exertions commenced and, really, never ceased, as though she were not in love with me but only my potential, as though I were some crude unformed raw matter, shapeless and pointless ore dredged up from the fog-enshrouded maw of my evidently primitive and clueless life and now about to be sculpted, painfully, savagely, constantly; and then, recoiling, I gawked at my reflection in the mirror, saw there some-one with eyes shrunken to pinpoints of abased being, skin mottled with a rash of self-loathing, mouth set into an expression like that of a mole unearthed by a steam shovel; and at that moment I saw that I was no one, had no reference point, my history erased. I could have sprung right then full-blown like a fly born in a bottle during a nineteenth-century lab experiment in spontaneous regeneration, or a character of Dickens's bursting suddenly into flame. A no one. A fictional effigy. A mannequin. A caricature.

There was no choice but to go on with the bad crazy haircut, try to make the best of my violation. Besides, I told myself, who would care anyway? I'm a writer, a thinker—though recently dis-covered to be one without a soul, who'd lost it in a devil's trade for love—now I'd go about posing as an eccentric existential thinker rather than what I was: a hostage to madness, hers, mine.

I would feel similarly as a child with my mother, who, like

Lena, had a foreign accent, who, like Lena, was obsessively, brutally critical. But who was also, like Lena, beautiful—or at least had been so in my early childhood when I'd stand transfixed before a hand-colored photograph of my mother bared to the cleavage, looking like a movie star, and I so utterly in love with who she once had been.

In turn, Lena treated me like a difficult child. But as a young child I had not been hard to manage. Until about the age of twelve I did exactly as bidden. Later, though, when I discovered that it was not typical to have the living daylights beat out of one, to be punched in the face, whipped with a wire hangar or heavy-buckled belt, or to take shattering near-bone-smashing blows from a heavy wooden rolling pin about the arms, particularly the forearms and elbows, I rebelled ferociously, viciously, with tempest fury, with a mouth so foul that my parents would end up locking themselves into the bedroom rather than endure yet another stream of filthy vilification. Really, the abuse stopped only when I became even more abusive than her. I stopped short of physical violence, but I threatened—and once, in a fit of blind rage, I punched my mother in the chest, which sent her flying against the wall. The self-destructive self-loathing that ensued from that event was delicious; it fueled acts of behavior so wild that my craziest friends feared me, and all of it was driven by an almost-pleasurable sense of indescribable remorse. Yes, that background explains all my interactions with Lena, and in fact every relationship I ever endured. In the end, she won. She defeated me. From her no successful revenge could be exacted. I was slavishly and deathlessly addicted to her, devoted and fully prepared to perish on the pyre of her love, like some traditional Indian wife. The legacy of this sad love affair—a blighted landscape extending from Innsbruck to Manhattan—was not only submission but black resignation to the sheer impossibility for me, for anyone, I suspect, to have and keep love. In the end, I lost everything, again. The wheel turned through one defeat after another, one sickening failure after the next, until finally there was nothing left, and she vanished, and then I vanished, into tears. And today, I live silently in dread.

Chapter 35

Now, I am alone at the end of my world. San Francisco as I knew it has died at the hands of ruthless realtors and callow Silicon Valley billionaires. Misguided love flipped me out of there into New York City but here it's no different, the local papers filled with death-knell op eds about the downfall of the city, the destruction of urban culture, the country ruled by a dictator, the ruin of America, which has become a drunken fascistic playground for the spoiled and worthless progeny of callow millionaire-followers of an illegitimate president.

I travel still. Israel. France. Britain. Holland. Anywhere but Germany. I have sought high and low for a quiet place to write, to no avail. When in New York City, I sit in Housing Works Bookstore Cafe surrounded by people who simply cannot, will not, shut up. It is so now. In the corner, a volunteer strumming a ukulele performs to young mothers and toddlers, clapping, talking, singing ceaselessly, her loud bland voice brimming with cutesy enthusiasm.

"And the horn on the buses goes beep beep beep all over town!" they sing cheerily amid shelves supporting books that bear the frowning, imperious visage of President Trump. The miserable nursery rhyme of our tyrannical kindergarchy of a world shrieks and claps in my brain. From the bloody sands of Syria to the soulless skyscrapers of Manhattan I see no hope, feel no hope—there is nowhere for anyone to go, flee to, to find Truth. There is no Truth. The death of Truth is the truth of Death. I feel murderously alone yet so sad, immobilized by loss, helpless to instigate change, incite rebellion, even in the end to generate some great and tragic work of art, which code-besotted digitized zombie Millennials won't read anyhow. Still, one must try, write in the face of Facebook, Twitter, Tinder, Zinger, and Shiner, though assuredly whatever one spits out will prove to be little more than irrelevant junk. And the mouth of the writer goes shit, shit, shit, all around the town. And the voice of the prophet goes doom, doom, doom all around the town.

Some last spurts and groans of self-help reflection, pop psychological and spiritual memorandums to the vast indifference, in order to underscore the aching sense of shameful failure, loss, and dread of the future that inhabit me—for I now exist as the proverbial warning of how Fate, bad choices, and a raging longing heart can undo the finest soul. Lena has made of me—caffeine-soaked, hunched over schoolboy composition notebooks, journaling furiously—a heartbroken parody of regret. For loss now ticks in my brain, loss, loss, loss; and loss is now the second hand of heartbreak; and as I sit now, hours later, at dusk, on a bench on a sun-painted traffic island in the middle of Broadway, staring blindly at Time, patiently awaiting the last tick of the doomsday clock, a black puddle of ashen pigeons moils about my shoes, while swarms of siren-screaming police cars rumble ominously over unsecured manhole caps; and though my ears are polluted by the self-absorbed and self-righteous homicidal glee of shrieking high school students, I try, try so very hard, to find words to depict to within five hundredths of a decimal point what heartbreak feels like, but can't seem to; no, I haven't really managed to convey that, have I, which angers me as so unfair—that one can suffer as I have, endure what I did, and yet remain utterly inchoate before the grief that throbs throughout the body and brain—an exhausting and revolting panorama of hysterical hope and convulsing tears, painted in murals of disquieting memory which appear to the mind as from nowhere, some of these images as high as the clouds and filled with vast expanses of blowing wind-filled trees in which I see her small dark-cloaked and shawl-wrapped figure recede, like some widow picking through the landscape of winter battle, searching for the corpse of her spouse, perhaps to see if some rubles remain hidden in the special pocket she had sewn in the lining and that only she knows of—searching for something, but what I no longer know, and I realize that really I never knew and never will; I'll never know what Lena's love was, how it felt to her, or if it was truly love at all or just some other pointless and incurable illness, a pathology freed of all social constraint, all history—a madness in a mad mind and from which she'd awaken now and then, terrified, to realize that either she had never loved me or anyone, or that she loved only me all along and lost me irrevocably, abandoned me. I do not know what my love meant, if love it was. I want to call it a perversion, myself a pervert. But is that so? Am I no more than that? Were we, Lena and I, only monsters, no more?

But when did monsters, true monsters, ever cry so much for the loss of each other? For I know that somewhere she weeps, as I do, for something that never should have been and yet had to be.

Perhaps the idea was unwittingly to isolate oneself into such an awful state of crushing helplessness and loneliness that finally any human interface will seem to have meaning, a purpose. But I have not yet reached that state of final grace.

Instead, as always, I am now awake late at night in a city—for I am still traveling to cities—where there is always someone awake.

Innsbruck, Graz, Salzburg, Zurich, Vienna, Tel Aviv,
San Francisco, New York City
July 14, 2018

About the Author

ALAN KAUFMAN, the Bronx-born son of a French-Jewish Holocaust survivor, is a writer, memoirist, and poet who is often compared to Jack Kerouac, Henry Miller, Hubert Selby Jr., and Ernest Hemingway, another soldier turned writer. He is the author of two critically acclaimed memoirs, *Jew Boy* and *Drunken Angel*, and a novel, *Matches*, based on his experiences as an Israeli combat soldier. He also edited four ground-breaking anthologies: *The Outlaw Bible of American Poetry*, *The Outlaw Bible of American Literature* (coedited with Barney Rosset), *The Outlaw Bible of American Essays*, and *The Outlaw Bible of American Art*.

Raised in the Bronx, he moved to Israel in the late 1980s and served for three years with the Israel Defense Forces. Returning to New York City, he enrolled for his MFA at Columbia and then relocated to San Francisco. In San Francisco he helped build the community of performance poets at Café Babar, led the 1993 SF Poets Strike, organized WORDLAND: The antifascist Spoken Word Ballroom (1993), and in 2011 launched the Free University of San Francisco. Kaufman emerged as a central figure in the Jewish countercultural movement, coediting *It's the Jews! A Celebration of New Jewish Visions* in 1995 with Danny Shot, and editing the controversial and groundbreaking magazine *DAVKA: Jewish Cultural Revolution*. He still resides in San Francisco and lives with Sloane, his new two-year-old rescue dog.